11/18

CRA

KT-461-542

WITHDRAWN

Alaskan Holiday

Debbie Macomber is a number one *New York Times* bestselling author and one of today's most popular writers with more than 170 million copies of her books in print worldwide. In addition to fiction, Debbie has published two bestselling cookbooks; numerous inspirational and nonfiction works; and two acclaimed children's books.

The beloved and bestselling *Cedar Cove* series became Hallmark Channel's first dramatic scripted television series, *Debbie Macomber's Cedar Cove*, which was ranked as the top programme on US cable TV when it debuted in summer 2013. Hallmark has also produced many successful films based on Debbie's bestselling Christmas novels.

Debbie Macomber owns her own tea room, and a yarn store, *A Good Yarn*, named after the shop featured in her popular *Blossom Street* novels. She and her husband, Wayne, serve on the Guideposts National Advisory Cabinet, and she is World Vision's international spokesperson for their *Knit for Kids* charity initiative. A devoted grandmother, Debbie lives with her husband in Port Orchard, Washington (the town on which her *Cedar Cove* .... Florida.

B000 000 024 9580

ABERDEEN LIBRARIES

Also by Debbie Macomber available in Arrow

Debbie Macomber

Alaskan Holiday

arrow books

3 5 7 9 10 8 6 4 2

Arrow Books
20 Vauxhall Bridge Road
London SW1V 2SA

Arrow Books is part of the Penguin Random House group of companies whose
addresses can be found at global.penguinrandomhouse.com.

Penguin
Random House
UK

Copyright © Debbie Macomber 2018

Debbie Macomber has asserted her right to be identified as the author
of this Work in accordance with the Copyright, Designs and Patents Act 1988.

First published in Great Britain by Arrow Books in 2018

www.penguin.co.uk

A CIP catalogue record for this book is available from the British Library.

ISBN 9781784758752

Typeset in 12/17 pt Adobe Garamond Pro by Jouve (UK), Milton Keynes
Printed and bound in Great Britain by Clays Ltd, Elcograf S.p.A.

MIX
Paper from
responsible sources
FSC   FSC® C018179
www.fsc.org

Penguin Random House is committed to a
sustainable future for our business, our readers
and our planet. This book is made from Forest
Stewardship Council® certified paper.

To Robert Macomber
Author, cousin, friend
And his wonderful wife,
Nancy Glickman

October 2018

Dear Friends,

No doubt there's something special about Alaska. Those who choose to live in the forty-ninth state are rugged individuals. I once read that in Alaska, the men are men and so are the women. It's also said that for single women in Alaska, your odds are good, but the goods are odd. Okay, enough with the jokes.

After the popularity of *Starry Night*, my publisher asked that I consider another story set in Alaska. It didn't take me long to come up with an idea set in the Far North. I'm particularly fond of that part of Alaska. Years ago, Wayne and I flew past the Arctic Circle doing research for a series of books I wrote back in the 1990s. We landed in a small town called Bettles and spent the day in this tiny Arctic town so I could get a firsthand taste of life on the tundra. It's a trip both of us hold close to our hearts.

My hope is that you'll fall in love with Palmer and Josie. Josie has her life planned, and it doesn't include finding love, especially with a man living in the Far North. She has goals, dreams, and plans for her future—with an opportunity of a lifetime waiting for her in Seattle. Palmer has plans, too, which include making

Josie his wife. And Jack! I trust he'll keep you laughing. Oops. I tend to get ahead of myself. You haven't turned the pages yet, but you will now. Sit back, relax, and immerse yourself in their story. At some point while you are reading, I hope you close your eyes and hear the crackling sounds of the Northern Lights.

As always, I enjoy hearing from my readers. You can reach me through Facebook, Instagram, or Twitter, or through my website, debbiemacomber.com. If you prefer, you can write me at P.O. Box 1458, Port Orchard, WA 98366.

The very warmest of regards,

Debbie Macomber

Alaskan Holiday

CHAPTER ONE

Palmer

"Are you gonna propose to Josie or not?" Alicia demanded.

I closed my eyes. It felt as if my heart was doing cartwheels inside my tightening chest.

"Palmer, did you hear me?"

"I heard you just fine." I knew it was a mistake to call my sister. Alicia wasn't one to hold back on sharing her opinion. She knew how I felt about Josie, and as my big sister, she was determined that I not let Josie leave town without letting her know how I felt about her.

"Then answer the question. Are you going to tell Josie you're in love with her?"

My sister and I had been raised in Alaska in a tiny

town above the Arctic Circle. We were homeschooled, so I didn't have a lot of the exposure and experiences most kids get for social interaction. I wouldn't give it up for anything, though, except for my lack of certain skills. Alicia made it sound easy to lay one's heart out on the chopping block with the big chance of it getting axed.

The problem is, I've never been anything even close to what one would consider romantic. I leave that to those city boys. I am a man, an Alaskan man; fancy, romantic words are as unfamiliar to me as a pumpkin-spice latte. I'll admit, when it comes to sweeping a woman off her feet, I'm about as dense as a guy can get, and I'll certainly never be the kind of man who recites poetry. Living up here in the Alaskan wilderness doesn't help. Ponder is miles from what most people would consider civilization. Northeast of Fairbanks and close to the Far North region of Alaska, Ponder has a population that swells to three hundred in-season when the lodge is in operation. In the wintertime, these numbers drop to a few hearty men and women, and only a handful of families.

Alicia reminded me that it was now or never. I could do without the clichés, especially when my gut was in knots. Even the thought of telling Josie that I loved her and wanted her to stay in Ponder had me breaking into a cold sweat. This felt worse than the case of flu I had last year.

Although the fishing and hunting lodge brought in a fair amount of traffic in-season, single women were few and far between here in Ponder. The only women I'd happened to meet in the last several years were those employed by the lodge, or those I met on my infrequent trips into Fairbanks. Most of the lodge employees were college students and so flighty and immature that I didn't pay any attention to them.

All that changed when Josie Avery arrived.

She was in her mid-twenties and had been hired on at the lodge as the chef for the season, which ran from May through the end of October. The minute I saw her, I knew she was different. The first thing I noticed was that her phone didn't come attached to her hand. The next time I saw her, she was reading a book. She stopped me cold when she happened to glance up and smile at me. Her eyes brightened, and I swear I could have drowned in her warmth. The sunlight had broken through the trees and landed on her like a pot of gold at the end of a rainbow. Her hair was long and dark and flowed over her shoulders. She wore jeans and boots. I hardly know how to explain what happened in that very moment.

I know it sounds nuts, but I felt something physical, like someone had hit me. The impact was so hard and strong that I stumbled back a step.

From that time on she was it for me. It didn't take me long to learn that she was intelligent and sensible, and had a great sense of humor. I was comfortable with her in ways I had never been with any other woman. I found I could talk to her with an ease that I'd never felt before, even with my sister.

Okay, to be honest, it didn't hurt that Josie was beautiful. I mean, her beauty was hard to deny. She had pretty eyes and she was just the right size, not too skinny. One thing Alicia taught me a long time ago was that women didn't take kindly to men talking about their bodies. To top it all off, Josie was good at what she did, and the food at the lodge had never been better.

Jack Corcoran, the old geezer who supplied the game to the lodge, had started to eat dinner there nearly every night. We'd become friends over the years, and I would join him, something I hadn't done much of in the past, until Josie's arrival. The Brewsters, who owned and operated the Caribou Lake Lodge, noticed me stopping by for dinner, and guessed the reason for my more frequent visits. They purposefully set Josie's schedule to give us more time together in the evenings, allowing me to introduce her to the beauty of Ponder and the Alaskan wilderness. I'd taken her hiking and searching for the Alaskan blueberry. We'd stumbled upon the lowbush cranberry as well and were able to pick enough for a wonderful sauce she'd used with moose meat. Just recently we'd lain under the stars and watched the Northern Lights flash-dance green highlights across the sky. Josie had gasped at their beauty. I barely noticed the wonder of it all, unable to take my eyes off her.

We'd had such good times together, Josie and me. When Ponder held its annual fishing derby during the Fourth of July celebration, Josie, who had never fished before, caught the winning fish. Beginners luck, she claimed. I was thrilled for her.

Most of all, Josie and I enjoyed our short evening hikes. With up to twenty-two hours of daylight in the summer, there was always plenty of time to explore the tundra after she'd finished her duties at the lodge.

I found her company easy, which quickly led me to thinking about how good it would be if she made Ponder her home with me. I knew enough about Josie to realize we'd get along great; we already did. A man gets lonely and housebound when the weather reaches as low as fifty degrees below freezing. Now that I was closing in on my thirtieth birthday, it was time, as Alicia repeatedly reminded me, that I thought about marriage and starting a family of my own.

Jack didn't want to see Josie leave, either. Jack had lived in the area for so long, he'd become part of the scenery. If you went to the dictionary and looked up the word *sourdough,* most likely you'd see a photo of Jack, not only because of his appearance, but because he was the legend behind the sourdough starter that kept all of Ponder in homemade bread year-round. In addition to supplying the wild game, Jack had been hired on at the lodge as a hunting guide. He took parties into the wilderness, camping two and three days at a time, giving tourists a real Alaskan experience. In his spare time, he panned for gold, although he'd never struck it rich the way he'd hoped to.

Josie had wanted to try her hand at it, too, and we'd spent an entire day in a fruitless search. While we might not have dredged up any nuggets, I felt that I'd found my biggest treasure in her.

Jerry Brewster, who owned the lodge along with Marianne, his wife, specialized in fishing on the lake. When summer arrived, you'd find Jerry out on the water every day, as he knew all the best spots. The lake was a tributary of the Copper River, where some of the best salmon in the world could be found, and a great hunting area. Folks loved the expertise that both Jerry and Jack had, and paid a high price for the privilege of hunting and fishing with them. People would take the passenger ferry to get to and from the lodge during the fishing and hunting season—the only way in and out of Ponder unless you could afford a seaplane. Come winter, before the lake froze over, Jerry put the boat in storage, and those who were not going to stay for winter took the last passenger ferry out. After that, a ski-plane made infrequent stops at Ponder, landing on the frozen lake.

With only a few businesses and families in the vicinity, we had everything a small wilderness town needed, including two taverns and two churches. The town balanced itself out that way, I suppose. I loved the peace and quiet and had made a good life for myself on beautiful Caribou Lake in the small town of Ponder.

"Have you listened to anything I've said?" Alicia asked.

"Uh . . ."

"That's what I thought. In case you've forgotten, Josie is leaving for Seattle first thing in the morning."

Like I'd forget what day it was. I'd started to ask Josie to marry me a dozen times or more in the last couple days but could never get out the words that I wanted to say. Now it was down to the last night, down to practically the last minute.

"I know." Already I could feel the tension building up inside me.

"Are you seriously going to let her go?" my sister harped.

Much as I love Alicia and her two kids, I didn't need her to remind me that the clock was ticking away when it came to Josie and me. Pressuring me to make my move wasn't helping. Alicia was right about one thing, though. I shouldn't have put it off as long as I had, but my rationale was simple: I was afraid, and with good reason. Josie had plans; she had a job waiting for her in Seattle. She had friends and family there as well. While I loved her and wanted to make her my wife, I wasn't sure that was enough to convince her to stay. I'd put off popping the question until it was either propose now or watch her leave come morning.

Besides, the reason I'd waited this long was because I knew if I'd asked too soon, and she didn't accept, then it would have been awkward for both of us for the remainder of the time Josie had at the lodge. So I'd held off. It made sense at the time. Little did I realize how much pressure I was putting on myself to convince her to stay and to marry me by delaying it until the last night. I guess I'd hoped she'd be so madly in love with me that she wouldn't want to leave. If that was the case, it wouldn't be hard to convince her to stay.

"You have a lot to offer a woman, Palmer," Alicia continued, once again interrupting my thought process. "For all you know, Josie could be impatiently waiting for you to say something."

"I wish."

"Just do it. You love her, right? Make your move."

My move. That was a laugh. The most Josie and I had done was hold hands and kiss like it was the end of the universe. Those kisses rocked my world. And they were hot. Sizzling hot. I had to assume she enjoyed our kissing, too, because we both looked forward to the times we could be alone. I might not be a mind reader when it came to women, but I saw the light in Josie's eyes when we were together, and I could live on one of her smiles for a week or longer. We had spent hours together over the past six months, and outside of our individual jobs, we were inseparable. I had grown to love this woman, and I could only hope she felt the same.

Josie claimed my beard tickled her lips. I offered to shave it off for her. That was a mighty big sacrifice for me, but she shrugged and said it wasn't necessary. That made me think she wasn't open to sticking around longer than required, but I'd never know unless I asked.

"We're going for a walk after dinner," I told Alicia. "I plan on proposing then." It didn't help knowing that her suitcase was already packed. For the last week our conversations had revolved around her life in Seattle. It seemed she could hardly wait to get back. She talked endlessly about the job that was waiting for her. This was a huge opportunity for her. These chats weren't the most encouraging discussions for me. Every time Josie mentioned Seattle, my stomach tightened.

"Promise you'll call me afterward."

"Maybe." I wasn't making any such commitment. It all depended on how it went with Josie. If she turned me down, then I doubted I'd be in the mood to talk to anyone, including my persistent sister.

After my conversation with Alicia, I took time off to think everything through. I work as a master swordsmith, forging swords and other weapons from metal. I'd been working at my craft from the age of sixteen, when I became an apprentice. Because I was homeschooled, I'd earned enough credits to graduate early. College didn't interest me. I'm a man who needs to work with his hands, not just his brain.

Currently, I was creating a replica of a Civil War sword.

It was an important commission, as the job was bringing in more money than any other project to date. I was fortunate enough to make a living doing what I loved. I worked most days in my workshop with my forge, hammer, and anvil. My needs were simple, and my work had gained a growing notoriety.

Since this evening was my one last shot with Josie, I had to do it right. Because I got tongue-tied every time I attempted to bring up the topic, I figured my best chance was to write down what I wanted to say. That was the only way I could ensure that I didn't forget an important point.

I was sitting at the kitchen table with my dog, Hobo, an Alaskan husky, who was sleeping at my feet while I composed a list. I was about halfway through making my notes when Jack showed up. As usual, he didn't bother to knock.

Glancing up from the table where I sat in my kitchen, he looked like he'd lost his best friend.

"You okay?"

"No," Jack replied, pulling out a chair and sitting down across from me. "The lodge is closing."

"It closes every year, Jack. That's nothing new."

Jack shook his head. "But Josie . . . she's leaving. She's the best cook they've ever had here."

I never understood how Jack managed to keep his weight down. I swear my friend ate as much as a grizzly bear.

"She made the best moose stroganoff I've ever had."

For me, Josie's leaving meant losing a lot more than her great cooking. "Yup," I agreed.

"She baked me a blueberry pie as a farewell gift, using the leftover berries she'd frozen. I ate the whole pie already, and that's when it hit me that there'd be no more."

I'd been the one picking those blueberries with Josie. I never thought I'd enjoy wandering around the lake's edge picking berries. Then again, I was willing to do about anything if it meant I could spend time with her. I had it bad. Even now, with the deadline closing in on me, I couldn't bear the thought of her leaving. That made my growing list even more important. If ever there was a time I needed my wits about me, it was now.

"You gonna miss her, too, right?" Jack asked me.

"Yeah, I suppose." No need admitting more than necessary.

Jack frowned. "You do know that if you were to marry her, she'd be here full-time and could cook for us?"

"Us?" I arched my brows. I didn't like the idea of Jack thinking he could drop by for meals any time the mood struck him, but then that was Jack. He was clueless when it came to social etiquette. Knowing him as well as I did, he'd be stopping by daily.

"Well, yes," Jack countered. "Seems right you'd want to invite me over."

I snorted out loud. "Not happening."

Jack appeared offended by my rejection. "Did I or did I not share that elk meat with you?"

"One roast does not equate to a lifetime of free meals."

"And my sourdough starter, which I'd like to remind you is over a hundred and fifty years old," Jack added.

"Right." I was willing to admit that I appreciated the starter and routinely made good use of it. I ate sourdough pancakes almost every morning, thanks to Jack's starter.

"Then show a little appreciation, son."

It probably wasn't right to roll my eyes, but I couldn't help it. "No use arguing, Jack. It's highly likely that Josie will leave in the morning, along with the rest of the lodge staff." I hated being a pessimist, but at the rate this list was going, I was slowly coming to the realization that I didn't have a lot to offer to convince her to stay, compared to what she had in the big city.

Jack's eyes brightened and he sat up straight, ready to solve the world's problems. "Palmer, I wasn't joking. You should marry her."

I didn't argue with him, but I certainly wasn't telling Jack that I intended to propose that very evening.

"You want me to ask her for you?" Jack eagerly offered, his face glowing with the idea. "I'd propose to her myself, but you're the one she's been spending her time with most evenings. Don't get me wrong. If I were you, I'd marry her right quick."

"Ah . . ."

"Don't worry, I'll ask her for you."

"What?" I demanded. "Listen here, old man, if anyone does the asking, it'll be me. I don't need you or anyone else speaking on my behalf."

Looking lost and dejected, Jack's shoulders drooped, and he leaned back against the chair. "Likely I'd mess it up anyway. Asked a woman to marry me once before, and it didn't turn out like I'd hoped."

This caught my attention. "Oh?" Maybe I could get some hints on what *not* to do from Jack's failed proposal.

"Yup, I was as nervous as a beaver on the tundra. She didn't seem all that interested in my offer . . . think I must have said something to offend her."

"What happened?"

Jack shook his head, attempting to rid himself of the memory. He raised his hand to his face, rubbing his beard. "You might have trouble believing it, but I used to be a good-looking fella. I was in my thirties at the time and was thinking if I was going to start a family, I had better find myself a woman and get to work."

I'd been having the same thoughts myself, although I wasn't going to mention it to Jack, because then the whole town would know.

"Did she give you a reason for turning you down?"

"Actually, she didn't do a lot of talking after I proposed." A thoughtful, sad look came over him.

"Oh."

"I didn't even mind that she had no experience cooking wild game. Fact is, I was willing to overlook a lot of her faults, and told her so, thinking she'd appreciate my generosity."

"And how did that go over?"

He stroked his beard once again. "She took offense. Never quite understood why. It wasn't like she had men pounding down her door. I thought she'd be happy that I was willing to marry her."

"Was she a good cook?"

"Fair. She didn't seem to receive that observation of mine very well, either. Women are funny that way. I probably should have exaggerated my appreciation of her skills in the kitchen."

"Did you tell her you thought she was pretty?"

"Nope. Truth was she wasn't much to look at. I didn't mind, though."

I swallowed a smile. "You didn't mention that to her, did you?"

"Oh no. Knew better than that. Women need to think they're the light of a man's life."

"What else did you say?" Little did Jack know, I was taking mental notes.

Jack tapped his finger against his lips. "Been twenty years ago now, so I don't recall the exact words. Never had high expectations, seeing that the ratio of men to women wasn't in my favor living here in the Alaskan wilderness. I do remember that I told her that she was the best I could do."

I could only imagine how well *that* comment had gone over with the poor woman.

Jack shook his head. "Still don't know why she didn't accept my proposal."

"She say anything else?"

Jack snorted. "A big fat NO was all I got. Apparently, I'd read her wrong. I could have sworn she was sweet on me."

"You propose to anyone else?"

"Nope. Once was enough. A man can only take so much rejection, and I'd had my fill."

This I could understand. Jack had given up after that single rejection. Frankly, I couldn't see myself wanting to marry anyone other than Josie. And if Josie ended up turning me down, then I feared I'd be just like Jack years down the road, looking back and wondering where I'd gone wrong.

The more I thought about it, the more I realized how important it was to say whatever it was that Josie needed to hear if I was going to convince her to marry me. As sad as it was to admit, I could see myself making a mess of my proposal the same way Jack had done.

Jack sadly shook his head and exhaled slowly. "In the end it was probably for the best that Sally rejected me. Don't know that I'm the marrying kind. You and me are a lot alike, you know."

This was not encouraging news.

My eyes drifted down to the list in front of me, and my heart sank. I had the distinct feeling it was going to take a miracle of biblical proportions to get Josie to agree to be my wife.

CHAPTER TWO

Josie

The Caribou Lake Lodge was closing for the winter, and after six months in Ponder, I was sorry to leave. It'd been the longest time I'd ever spent away from my mother and the city of Seattle, where I'd been born and raised. The separation hadn't been easy, but I felt it was time well spent. It'd always been just my mom and me, and being apart had taught me valuable lessons about myself, lessons I hoped to take with me as I headed off to my first real job. As a sous-chef, I'd be working hand in hand with the head chef, creating menu items, plus training new staff, as well as keeping the kitchen organized and flowing. I'd been given the opportunity of a lifetime, working in a newly opened Seattle restaurant with Douglas Anton, a renowned chef. A career break like this didn't come along every day. For me, it was a dream come true. The culinary school I'd attended had recommended me for the position. Their faith in me was more than I could have dreamed. The only drawback was that I had to wait six months after graduation for the completion of Chef Anton's newest restaurant, which was why I happened to be in Alaska. This opportunity not only helped me to pass the time, but it also gave me the chance to do what I loved best: create recipes based on locally sourced ingredients.

Now it was the end of October, and time to return home and start my career. In the morning, the Brewsters, the remainder of the staff, and I would catch the last passenger ferry for the long ride down the lake to semi-civilization, before hopping on a small plane to Fairbanks, and from there, on to Seattle.

I was surprised at how well I'd acclimated to Alaska and to the lack of amenities, considering I'd grown up in a city where I'd had everything at my fingertips. Ponder had no shopping mall, theater, or Starbucks. Access to the Internet was only a recent addition in the past few years, and that had been a game-changer for everyone in town.

Alaska was beautiful. One of my favorite things to do was watch the eagles dive for fish in the lake. Jerry

Brewster, the lodge owner, entertained me with story after story of the eagles on Caribou Lake. One time he'd hooked a salmon and was reeling it in when an eagle swooped down and grabbed the fish and flew off with it. With the fish still attached to the line, Jerry attempted to reel it in, fighting the eagle for the salmon. While Jerry eventually won the battle, the eagle had left talon marks on the salmon's flesh.

Being a member of a small community took some getting used to, but I'd managed in short order. Life here was a stark contrast to that in Seattle or any big city. I especially enjoyed the way folks used any excuse they could find for a community gathering. There was the Midnight Sun Festival, which included a midnight baseball game, and yes, it was full sunlight at midnight. The Fourth of July Festival. The Chili Cook-off won by a young mother, Angie Wilkerson. I'd wished there'd been more time to get to know her, as I felt we could have been friends.

The longer I lived at the lodge, the more beauty I discovered each day. I could stare for hours at the night sky. Living in the city, I'd never truly seen stars the way I could in Alaska. I was left awestruck by how many were visible in the totally black sky, like diamond dust scattered across the heavens.

Of course, I'd been here through spring, summer, and early autumn, when the awesome splendor of all that was Alaska was evident every day. I'd been able to observe moose and caribou from afar, and even once saw a bear amble down the middle of town as if it was shopping day. Moments like those made me have no regrets for not having access to a Starbucks or a nail salon for almost six months. I'd more than survived this experience—I'd thrived here in Ponder. I wouldn't have thought it was possible when I'd arrived. Those first couple weeks in town, all I saw was what the little town *didn't* have. It wasn't long before I began to appreciate the abundance of all that it *did* have to offer.

And then there was Palmer Saxon. My heart grew heavy at the thought of saying good-bye to him and his constant companion, a big husky named Hobo. It would have been far too easy to fall totally in love with him. It was hard to think about leaving without my mind and my heart automatically returning to Palmer. It was going to be difficult—harder than I wanted to think about.

Palmer was the epitome of how one would define an Alaskan man.

Independent.

Self-sufficient.

Stubborn.

23

Rugged.

And a dozen other adjectives quickly came to mind. Just the thought of Palmer being outside of this world, and wearing a suit and tie, was enough to make me giggle. I couldn't picture him in anything other than his plaid flannel shirts and worn blue jeans. We'd grown close in the time I'd spent at the lodge. He was unlike any man I'd ever known. We'd never officially had a typical date, like dinner or a movie—and yet I felt like I knew him better than any of my friends back home. We'd spent virtually every day together since I'd been here. It wasn't going to be easy to leave. Thinking about Palmer weighed down my heart. Really, there was no future for us, I had reasoned to myself. I'd come to love Alaska, but I couldn't imagine spending the rest of my life here. Nor would Palmer ever be happy in a big city. The traffic alone would undo him.

As hard as it was to admit, it was unlikely I'd ever return to Ponder. It was best to let the relationship die before either of us had regrets. It saddened me. I knew I was going to miss Palmer dreadfully, but I was mature enough to accept that there was no other option than for me to leave come morning.

In addition to Palmer, I'd miss Jack, too. He was a good man, kind and gentle. Funny, too, although I don't think he realized it. Over the six months I'd spent at the lodge, he'd become like a father figure to me. My own father had died when I was only three years old in a construction accident before I had any memories of him. While Mom had occasionally dated over the years, there'd never been anyone serious.

Like Palmer, Jack was everything I'd listed as a true Alaskan man, and more. He'd worn the same shirt and pants the entire time I'd been working at the lodge. Apparently, he'd bought several sets of the same outfit and wore them repeatedly. He must have gotten a discount, was all I could think. That, or he couldn't be bothered with appearances.

The one thing continually on Jack's mind was food. He gushed with compliments over my cooking. I swear I could have fed him boxed macaroni and cheese and he'd say he'd never eaten anything better. The way he told it, I cooked like an angel. He repeatedly insisted that he'd never tasted food as good as what I served. I'm convinced he fed the same line to every chef who'd ever been at the lodge, but I had to say I enjoyed hearing it. When Jack wasn't guiding a hunting party or panning for gold, he found every excuse under the sun to hang around the kitchen with me. I enjoyed our talks—I was comfortable discussing my career, hopes, and goals with him. I liked to think that if my father had lived, we would've shared conversations like those I'd shared with Jack.

My suitcases were packed, and I was ready to leave when the ferry arrived, at about six in the morning. We were instructed to have our luggage in the lobby that night before heading to bed. Jerry had already pulled his boat out of the water and taken it across the lake for servicing and winter storage. Within a week, two at the most, the lake would freeze over. Most of the summer residents of Ponder had already departed for the winter, and it had become something of a ghost town. Only a few rugged souls remained behind, Palmer and Jack among them.

The knock on my door didn't surprise me. I figured it was Palmer, and I was right. Per our usual routine, he waited until the kitchen was clean and I was in my room before he stopped by.

"Hey," I said, smiling at him, doing my best to hide my heart. Seeing him, I realized that this was going to be harder than I'd thought it would be. We'd spent evenings together practically every night for the last six months. I'd truly enjoyed every minute with him and Hobo. I'd never had a relationship like this, nor had I ever felt as close emotionally to a man. I feared that in the future

I would compare everyone I dated to him, and everyone else would pale in comparison.

"You up for a walk?" he asked.

It was the same question he asked me every night.

"Sure." I looked around. "Where's Hobo?"

"I left him at the house."

That wasn't typical. Hobo was Palmer's shadow—he almost always joined us. I reached for a jacket as we headed out of the lodge. Evenings had become decidedly cooler now. There'd even been a hint of snow the day before, and more was forecasted. While it was only October, this part of Alaska typically had snow by this time, and I knew Seattle was already engulfed in the autumn rainy season.

I dressed warmly, being sure to use thick wool socks along with my boots. Because it was my last night, I didn't want to turn Palmer down, despite the frigid air. I could see my breath when we stepped outside.

"It's getting colder every day now," I commented, looking up at the sky on the off chance I'd get one last look at the Northern Lights before I departed. The aurora borealis was something to behold. Flashing streaks of purple and green shot across the night sky, the beauty of it taking my breath away every time. One of my favorite memories of my time in Alaska was lying on my back with Palmer beside me, holding my hand, while we looked up at the sky. I'd never felt closer to anyone.

"Winter's coming on," Palmer said, hands buried deep inside his coat pockets.

Just this morning, Jerry had mentioned that according to the *Farmers' Almanac*, this winter was forecasted to be one of the coldest on record. The lake had already started to freeze.

I tucked my arm around Palmer's elbow because of the uneven ground. All right, it was an excuse. I liked being close to Palmer, and because it was our last night together, this made it especially poignant.

We walked down the familiar path, and he was unusually quiet.

"Josie?"

"Yeah?"

He released my arm and reached inside his jeans pocket, removing a slip of paper. Then he turned toward the moonlight to read whatever was on it.

"You're beautiful," he read. "I want you to know when I look at you all I see is beauty."

Well, that was nice, although unexpected. "Thank you, Palmer."

He looked down at his list a second time. "I like that your teeth are white and straight, too."

Teeth? He liked my teeth? "Ah, thanks. I wore braces for almost two years. Mom couldn't afford an orthodontist bill, so she baked and sold cakes to pay for all the dental work I needed." My mother had made sacrifices throughout my entire childhood.

"I like your blue eyes, too."

I grinned and looked down at the ground. "They're brown, Palmer."

"They are? I could have sworn they were blue."

"Nope, always have been brown."

He inhaled so loudly I thought he might pass out. "You okay, Palmer?" He was acting so strangely.

Bracing his hand against the side of a tree, he hung his head.

He had me worried. "Are you okay?" I asked again, frowning. He looked decidedly uncomfortable. I was about to suggest we return to the lodge when he started to speak again.

"Yes," he barked. "I'm feeling just fine." He looked up and apologized. "I . . . I didn't mean to snap at you."

"It's okay. I'd hate for us to argue on my last night here. That happens, you know."

"What happens?" he asked, as he broke away from the tree and we continued our walk.

"I have a friend," I explained, hoping to ease the

awkwardness between us. "Her name is Jessie, you might have heard me mention her before."

"What about Jessie?"

"Her husband's in the Navy, stationed on an aircraft carrier. He's away up to eight months at a time. She told me that before he leaves port, they always seem to have a big fight. I know it sounds nuts, but she says it makes it easier for him to go and for her to be without him. They always make up, but it's a pattern they've fallen into."

"Oh?"

It sounded as though Palmer didn't have an inkling as to why I'd mentioned Jessie. "I was thinking, you know, that we should have a fight, because it would be easier for us to part ways in the morning."

Palmer didn't seem to hear me. Instead of responding, he looked down at the same piece of paper. "I've never met anyone who can cook as well as you, and still manage to stay in good shape."

I managed to swallow a laugh, because he appeared to be entirely serious. "Well, thank you, Palmer, but you know the saying about not trusting a skinny cook."

"I trust you, Josie," he insisted. "I don't want you to think that I don't."

"I know you trust me. It's just a joke people make,

Palmer." I couldn't figure out what on earth had gotten into him.

"Your hair smells good, too, like vanilla and strawberries."

"It's the shampoo I use," I explained. He *really* didn't look well. "Are you *sure* everything is all right, Palmer? You're acting strange."

"I'm fine. The way a woman smells is important to a man."

"Yes, I suppose it is. The way a man smells is important to a woman, too," I assured him.

"I routinely bathe," he rushed to tell me, as if it was vitally important that I know he had good hygiene.

"Yes, I'm sure you do."

"I don't put on any of that fancy cologne, though. That doesn't bother you, does it?"

"Not in the least." In all the months I'd been in Ponder, this was the oddest conversation I'd had with Palmer. I looked up, and his features were highlighted by the moonlight. Right away I noticed how pale he was. "Palmer, you *are* sick. It looks like you're about to throw up."

He leaned his back against a tree and closed his eyes. "I think I might."

Coming to stand next to him, I placed my hand on his shoulder. "Bend over and take in deep breaths."

He did as I suggested and noisily dragged oxygen into his lungs. His shoulders heaved with the effort.

"Let me walk you back to your cabin. Do you need water?"

"What I need," he grumbled, "is for this to be over."

He wasn't making sense. Wrapping my arm around his waist, I led him back the way we'd come, steering off the path toward his cabin. We hadn't gone more than a few feet when he stopped abruptly. He turned so that he was facing me and placed his hands on my shoulders. His grip was tight.

"I don't want you to go," he said, his eyes imploring mine.

"Don't worry, I'll stay in your cabin with you for a bit, until you're feeling better," I assured him.

"Not my *cabin*, Josie," Palmer corrected me. "I don't want you to leave *Ponder*."

That made absolutely no sense. "Not leave Ponder? But the lodge is closing for the winter." He knew this as well as I did. The lodge closed every winter.

"You can stay."

"No, I can't." What he was suggesting was utter nonsense. I couldn't begin to imagine what he was thinking. He knew I had a wonderful job waiting for me in Seattle; we'd talked about it multiple times.

"You like Alaska, don't you?"

"It was a challenge in the beginning, but yes, I like it. These past six months have been a great experience, one that I will always treasure."

His face relaxed. "Then you wouldn't mind staying? Winters can be rough, but after a few years you grow accustomed to the freezing temperatures and dealing with the cold. There's beauty here during the winter months that you won't find anyplace else in the world."

"I'm sure that's true."

"Then you'll stay?" He looked hopeful and eager.

"Palmer. The lodge is closing. What would I do with my time? I need to work to support myself. I have a whole other life waiting for me back in Seattle. My mom is there, my friends, plus I have a great opportunity to work for Chef Anton. You know all that. I don't understand what you want. In fact, this entire conversation isn't making the least bit of sense."

Palmer closed his eyes and then opened them again. His look was as serious as I'd seen. "You could cook for Jack and me. I've been giving this a lot of thought, and this is what I think you should do. I know this job is important to you, Josie, and remaining at the lake would be a big sacrifice on your part."

His eyes made direct contact with mine before he continued.

"I would consider moving to Seattle, but living in a city would never work for me."

"You'd move to Seattle just so I could *cook* for you?" I knew my way around a kitchen, but for him to turn his entire life upside down to take advantage of my culinary skills was nothing short of preposterous.

A determined look appeared on his face. "Well, of course. A husband needs to be with his wife."

"His WIFE?" I practically exploded. At some point I'd completely lost track of where this odd conversation was leading. "You're asking me to *marry* you?"

His gaze was warm and soft as he nodded his head, his eyes wide and sincere.

I placed my hand against my heart as I realized what Palmer had been trying to say. So *this* was why he'd started with all those silly compliments.

"Well, Josie?" he asked, his voice full of anticipation. "Will you?"

"You want to *marry* me?" I asked him again, to be certain I understood him.

"Yes," he continued. "I've probably made a mess of this. I apologize, Josie, I should never have listened to Jack. He was sure if I told you how beautiful you are that it would sway you, so I tried to find ways to let you know it was more than just your looks and your cooking. I've never been in love before. Never spent as much time with a woman as I have with you. Being with you makes me happy. I want you to marry me more than anything. Put me out of this misery and say you'll marry me and live here with me in Ponder."

"Oh Palmer." I honestly thought I might break into tears. It took awhile to gain my composure before I answered. Pressing my hands against the sides of his face, against his beard, I tried my best to explain. "Palmer, as much as I appreciate everything you've said"—my voice caught and cracked as I spoke—"I can't. I . . . just can't. I'm so sorry."

He hung his head in defeat and slowly exhaled. "I was afraid you'd say that."

"My life is in Seattle."

He nodded, acting like he wasn't surprised that I'd turned him down.

"It's always been my mom and me, and I can't leave her, Palmer. I'm all she has." We were close, always had been. While my friends had gone through tough times with their parents, I could honestly say I never had. My mother was everything to me. She and I had connected almost every day while I was in Ponder. Well, nearly every day. She seemed to be unusually busy this last summer, and there'd been a two- or three-day span when I hadn't been able to reach her. Being away from her had been the hardest part of living in Alaska.

"Is there anything I can offer that would tempt you to change your mind?" he asked.

My throat felt raw with the effort to hold back tears, so rather than speak, I shook my head.

The silence between us was excruciating.

"Then it's a definite no?"

I felt dreadful, sick at heart. "I'm sorry."

"Please don't apologize."

I couldn't help it. It took every ounce of self-control I possessed to maintain my composure. More than anything, I hated disappointing Palmer. It hurt me to reject him. And the truth was, I was tempted, sincerely tempted. I yearned to tell him how badly I wished things could be different, but it would be pointless. There might be a chance for us if he lived in Seattle, but it went without saying that I'd never ask that of him. Palmer was as much a part of Alaska as the rugged wilderness that surrounded the lake. He'd be completely out of his element and totally unhappy in the city.

Unexpectedly, Palmer pulled me into his arms and hugged me close. I wanted him to kiss me. He didn't. I felt him take a slow, deep breath before he gently took hold of my shoulders.

"Have a good life, Josie."

He held on to me a bit longer before he turned away. Without looking back, he walked toward his cabin.

I watched him go and my heart sank. Part of me wanted to holler and say I'd marry him, but I knew I couldn't. The life and career that I had worked so hard for was back in Seattle, not in Ponder.

How long I stood in the dark, I couldn't say. Eventually, I made my way back to the lodge. Both Jerry and Marianne Brewster were standing by the huge rock fireplace that dominated the lobby. The last guests had departed the day before, so only the Brewsters and a few staff members remained.

Jerry and Marianne looked at me expectantly, acting like they'd been waiting for my return and that I had some announcement to make.

Jack was there, too. When I entered the room, the older man slowly stood and stared at me with anticipation.

"Well?" he asked. "You gonna marry Palmer or not?"

I stood frozen, not more than two feet inside the door. It seemed everyone knew Palmer was going to propose tonight—everyone except me.

Sadly, I shook my head. Tears began to fall down my cheeks.

"He should have let me do the asking," I heard Jack say, as I quickly headed back to my room.

"Josie, be sure to put your suitcases in the lobby before you head to bed," Jerry called after me.

I nodded, though I was in such a hurry I doubt anyone saw.

CHAPTER THREE

Josie

I woke in the dark, warm and comfortable. Stretching my arms above my head, I yawned, surprised the alarm hadn't woken me, especially since I'd spent a miserable night tossing and turning, unable to sleep.

The last time I'd looked at the clock, it was close to three in the morning, and I had only two and a half hours to get some sleep before I had to be up to catch the ferry. My head was spinning after Palmer had proposed, and I couldn't get to sleep. So I crawled out of bed and took one of those aspirins that had a sleeping aid in it. Quite honestly, it had surprised me that I'd managed to fall asleep at all, even with that bit of help. Rolling over, I glanced at the clock on my bedside table and froze.

I looked again and blinked hard.

8:30 a.m.

That couldn't be right. No possible way.

The ferry was scheduled to leave Ponder at six this morning. Throwing off the covers, I jumped out of bed and flung open the door to my room.

"Marianne!" I shouted.

My voice echoed down the hallway and returned to me, empty. The lodge was eerily silent. They *couldn't* have left without me—Marianne and Jerry wouldn't do that to me. They knew I had to be back in Seattle for my new job.

I raced into the kitchen, certain I'd find them drinking coffee and making jokes about me oversleeping. If not the Brewsters, then *someone* must have stayed behind. Anyone.

But the kitchen was dark, cold, and, worst of all . . . vacant.

My heart was pounding like war drums by the time I returned to my room. Before going to bed, I'd purposefully laid out my traveling clothes next to my packed suitcases and carefully set my alarm.

My alarm. Had I forgotten to set my alarm? No, of course not. I wouldn't forget something like that. I remembered doing it. I grabbed my phone to verify that I had it set to wake me, and instantly realized my mistake. I'd set

40

it, all right. For five-thirty in the afternoon, instead of the morning.

Groaning, I quickly got dressed in my jeans and sweatshirt and raced around the lodge, my heart in my throat, looking for . . . I didn't know what I was looking for. Maybe some sort of evidence that I hadn't been abandoned and left behind.

It took several minutes before I found the note Marianne had left me.

Josie,

I repeatedly knocked on your door, but there was no answer, and you hadn't brought out your suitcases, so I assumed you'd had a change of heart about accepting Palmer's proposal and decided to stay in Ponder after all.

Congratulations from the bottom of our hearts! Jerry and I wish you both every bit of happiness. Count on working for us next season, as we would love to have you back.

Marianne

She'd wrongly assumed that I had decided to ditch the opportunity of a lifetime to work with the chef of my dreams. She believed I'd stayed behind to marry Palmer.

Was she nuts? Or was I?

As drawn as I was to Palmer, I couldn't marry him. I'd stayed up half the night going over every conceivable way to make our relationship work and I couldn't think of one. Yet Marianne had apparently believed that I had second thoughts. That sleep aid had worked its dark magic, and I'd never heard Marianne knock on my door.

A sob rose up in my throat. I'd been left behind. Abandoned.

The ferry that had departed this very morning was the last one out of Ponder until next spring. The last to travel across Caribou Lake before it froze over for the long Alaskan winter.

Panic filled me as I grabbed my jacket and shot out of the lodge, racing to the dock, hoping against hope that I wasn't too late. My footsteps echoed through the morning stillness as dawn broke over the horizon. By the time I reached the water, my heart was pounding in my throat. Bending forward, I placed my hands on my hips and stared into the distance. As far as the eye could see was water. There wasn't even a ripple on the lake, letting me know that it had been a long time since the boat had left the dock. Ice had already started to form against the lake's edge, and to complicate everything, it had started to snow.

Not knowing what else to do, I returned to the lodge and my room. I sank onto the end of my bed and struggled to hold back tears while I reviewed my options, of which there seemed to be shockingly few. This was Palmer's fault.

Looking to place the blame fully on his shoulders, I headed out the door once more and practically ran to his cabin, eager to confront him for causing this fiasco. His workshop was attached to the house and I let myself in without knocking, not that he was likely to hear me with all the noise in his shop. Hobo's bed was in the corner of the room. He lifted his head when I stepped inside but then lowered his chin to his paw as if he'd been expecting me all along.

I found Palmer pounding away on a red-hot blade of steel, what looked like a long sword, worthy of a Japanese warrior. I'd never met a swordsmith before Palmer and had found his work fascinating. Over the last six months, I'd spent a lot of time in his workshop and learned a lot about what he did. He was a true artist.

Stopping just inside the door to catch my breath, I noticed Palmer had on a work shirt. Even without the sleeves rolled up, I could see the bulging muscles of his upper arms. He loved what he did, and from what the Brewsters had told me, he was one of the best in the country. His swordsmith work was highly sought by people all around the world. Because Palmer was passionate about his craft, I felt that he, of all people, would understand why I couldn't give up this opportunity to work with Chef Anton. There had to be a way to get back to Seattle. If not, I didn't know what I was going to do.

It took him a minute to notice me. When he did, he froze, his hammer raised. At first all he did was stare at me. Setting the hammer aside, he shifted the protective eyewear to the top of his head, his face beginning to glow as a slow smile came over it.

"You stayed," he said, in a voice that told me he found it hard to believe I was still in Ponder.

"No, I *didn't* stay," I insisted, overwhelmed by my predicament.

Palmer blinked and frowned before I realized what I'd said.

"Not by choice, that is," I quickly amended.

His brow folded into a deep frown. "Are you saying you haven't changed your mind about marrying me?"

"I overslept and missed the boat, and furthermore," I said, struggling not to weep, "this is all your fault."

"Mine?"

"You had to ruin everything and propose. You had to know that my heart would say yes and that my head would say no, and now . . . now you need to help me get to Seattle." The least Palmer could do was find me a way out of Ponder.

He kept staring at me as if I'd lost my mind. "Why is it *my* fault that you missed the ferry?"

"You proposed . . . and I couldn't sleep . . . then I took an aspirin with a sleep aid . . . When I did . . . I didn't hear anything . . . Marianne's note said she knocked . . . but I didn't wake up."

Palmer said nothing and continued to look at me. He seemed to be expecting more of an explanation.

"Aren't you going to say anything?"

He cocked his head to the side. "Does your hair always look like that in the morning?"

I hadn't taken time to brush it, and I probably looked like someone who'd crawled out of a deep, dark cave. Not that I cared, and besides, Palmer should realize now wasn't the time to point that out.

"Palmer Saxon, is that all you have to say to me? My life is in Seattle and I need you to find a way to get me there."

He continued to stare at me like I'd lost my mind. "I don't know what you think I could do."

"I *need* to get back to Seattle," I fairly shouted at him. There had to be a way, and he was the only person I knew who could help me. The restaurant would be opening in only two weeks and I was supposed to be there to get everything organized. This was my entire future—my life.

He shrugged. "I wish I could help you, Josie, I really do, but the ferry left, and that was the last one of the season."

I couldn't believe what I was hearing. "Do you mean to say you won't help me?"

"I don't know what I can do." He lowered his protective eye gear and reached for the tongs that would put the metal into the fire again.

Anger hit me like a boxer's glove directly in the stomach, and I stomped my foot. "This was exactly what you wanted, isn't it? This must be a dream come true for you. You're overjoyed that I'm stuck in Ponder. Admit it, Palmer."

He shrugged, unwilling to own up to the truth. "Can't say it upsets me. Wish you were happier about it, but I figure you'll adjust in time."

"I am not adjusting to anything," I flared, growing angrier by the minute. "Don't you worry, Palmer, I'll find a way out of here if it's the last thing I do." My career was at stake, and from the look on his face, Palmer couldn't be more pleased. Clenching my hands into tight fists at my sides, I whirled around and headed back to the lodge, determined to find a way home.

Not more than a few steps away from Palmer's workshop, I met up with Jack. The older man's face lit up with a smile bright enough to rival the Northern Lights.

"You're marrying Palmer. I knew you'd reconsider, Josie."

I was about to explain the situation when he interrupted.

"What's for dinner?"

"I'm. Not. Cooking." I had other things I needed to be doing. The last thing on my mind was planning a menu for the week.

"Sure, sure, you need a couple nights off. I understand. I'll make do, but it'll be hard." His eyes sparkled, like a new thought had come to him. "If you don't want to cook dinner, how about putting together something for lunch? No need to make it fancy. Homemade soup, a few sandwiches, and a dozen home-baked cookies should do me up just fine."

"Jack," I said, through gritted teeth. "Listen to me and listen good. I'm not cooking because I'm leaving Ponder as soon as I can find a way to get out of here."

He frowned, because clearly, he didn't understand. He had the same strange look that Palmer had when I announced I hadn't stayed behind to marry him.

"The ferry has already left."

He said this like I wasn't already aware of the fact. "I know. I overslept. Now I need to get home, one way or another."

"Oh."

There was a wealth of meaning in that lone two-letter word. His shoulders sagged, and a defeated, forlorn look came over him. For half a second, I felt the urge to hug and comfort him, until I realized I had several phone calls to make. There had to be a way to get back.

Marching past Jack, I returned to the lodge and went directly to the reception desk, where Marianne kept all the important phone numbers. While a good portion of my time had been spent in the kitchen, I'd learned a lot about the running of the lodge from Marianne. She'd had me make phone calls for her on occasion, so I knew where to look for the information.

I wasn't encouraged.

The first number I dialed was to the company that owned and operated the ferry on Lake Caribou. I was quickly informed that the early-morning run was the last of the season.

End of discussion.

So much for that idea. I'd hoped they would take pity on me and make one last run. The woman on the other end of the line was sympathetic, but there was nothing more she could do.

Not one to easily quit, I next searched for the number of a seaplane operation. Marianne had only one listed, which meant this was a company she trusted and could rely on. I explained my situation and asked the price of what it would cost to have a pilot fly in and take me to Fairbanks.

When the man on the other end of the line gave me the quote, I gasped. "But that's outrageous," I protested.

"Seaplanes aren't cheap, young lady."

"Obviously."

"You want to book the flight? 'Cause if that's what you want, you'd better do it soon. Caribou Lake is already showing signs of freezing over."

"Ah . . . not yet. I need to explore a couple other options first." I didn't exactly know what those might be, but I wasn't giving up yet. Before I spent a big chunk of what I'd managed to save over the past six months, I wanted to be sure there wasn't another way out of Ponder.

"You saying you want to *ponder* your decision?" he asked and laughed, thinking himself clever.

I didn't laugh. "Thank you for your help," I said, and ended the call.

I glanced out the lodge windows and noticed that the snow was falling hard now, thick flakes coming down so fast my vision was blurred.

Perfect. Just perfect. I had to wonder what other sucker punch life was going to throw at me.

Sitting at the desk, I reviewed the last two phone conversations and released a sigh of frustration and defeat. I'd need to tell my mother what happened, knowing I was sure to get the support and sympathy I so badly needed.

She answered on the second ring. "Mom," I cried, struggling not to break into tears. "I missed the boat."

"Figuratively or literally?" she asked.

"Literally. Palmer proposed, and I overslept." I blurted out the whole story and barely took a breath in between.

When I was finished, the other end of the line was silent. "Mom? Did you hear what I said?"

"Every word. Sounds to me like you're stuck in Ponder."

"Mom, I can't stay here. I need to get back to Seattle." What I wanted from her were ideas. My mother always seemed to have a way of making the best out of the worst situation imaginable. And in case she'd forgotten,

I proceeded to list all the reasons it was necessary to return as soon as possible, including the opportunity to work alongside Chef Anton.

"Palmer asked you to marry him?" she asked, as if she hadn't heard a word I'd said. "You've mentioned his name a number of times, but I didn't realize things were serious. He sounds like a nice young man."

"Mom!" I cried out in frustration. "You don't seem to understand the gravity of my situation. I *have* to get home. Can't you think of *something*?"

"How did he propose? Did he get down on one knee?"

Although I was annoyed and at my wits' end, I smiled at the thought of Palmer's strange proposal the night before. "No, he told me I had straight teeth." In retrospect, I realized that was his convoluted way of letting me know he loved my smile.

As I suspected she would, Mom laughed. "That reminds me of when your father asked me to marry him. He was nervous and edgy, and finally he said he didn't want to do it. When I asked him what it was he didn't want to do, he looked at me with love in his eyes and said he didn't want to live the rest of his life without me."

"Oh Mom," I whispered. "That's so romantic." A whole

lot more romantic than Palmer saying he liked my straight teeth or that my hair smelled like my shampoo.

"Your father was about the least romantic man I've ever met, to be honest," Mom continued. "But he loved me, and he adored you. Well, this isn't about me. I'm sure there's a way for you to find your way home."

"I'm sure there is, too," I repeated, feeling more confident now.

I had to believe she was right. I didn't know how Mom had managed to calm me. She'd always been able to settle me down.

No matter what, I was headed back to where I had to be. All I had to do now was think it through sensibly and calmly. I had to believe that where there was a will, there was a way.

More encouraged after talking to my mom, I told her I loved her, ended the call, and released a slow sigh. I was determined, even if it meant getting out of here by hiring a sled-dog team.

CHAPTER FOUR

Palmer

Jack burst into my workshop like he was urgently seeking shelter from an air raid. "Did you hear?" he cried excitedly. "Josie missed the boat!" Hobo walked over to greet him, and Jack absently patted his head.

"I heard." I hadn't taken time to digest the news just yet. Having her remain in Ponder was both a blessing and a curse. Eventually she would find a way out, and having her go would be even harder. Still, she was stuck in town for now, and I couldn't help but be pleased, although I knew she was angry and frustrated.

"Don't you see?" Jack insisted impatiently. "It's our opportunity to convince her to marry you. God gave you a second chance to win her over, so don't waste it,

Palmer. You hear me?" He sounded more like a drill sergeant issuing orders than the old sourdough I'd come to consider a friend.

I didn't want to discourage him, but from the way I saw it, Josie couldn't get away from me fast enough. When I first saw her standing in my workshop this morning, it felt like my heart had swollen to twice its normal size. For one crazed second, I thought she'd reconsidered and decided to marry me. It didn't take her long to set the record straight.

"She's determined to leave," I told Jack, going about my business.

"Maybe she wants to leave *now,* but that won't last if we play our cards right. Don't you see? Josie missing the ferry gives us the time we need to get her to reconsider your proposal."

Jack was losing what was left of his mind. "I don't have anything to offer her. She made it clear what she wants, and it isn't me. In fact, she blames me that she's stuck here." Still hadn't figured out how that could be. I wasn't the one who'd overslept. Far as I could see, this problem fell squarely on her.

Jack continued to stare at me, looking long and hard, as if it would help him understand me better. "You have to admit you're happy she's here. It doesn't matter how it happened; it happened. It was like an act of God. You know, like an earthquake or a volcano erupting."

"It wasn't any act of God," I corrected him. "It was a mistake, plain and simple. Josie overslept."

Jack adamantly shook his head. "That's not the way I see it, and you shouldn't, either. You've been given more time to get her to fall in love with you. Don't waste it."

As much as I wanted to accept his advice, I was afraid to have my heart battered a second time.

"Palmer?" Jack refused to give up.

"I'll do what I can," I agreed, but I didn't know what more that would be. I'd already proposed to Josie, given it all I had. She'd rejected me. Being left behind in Ponder really had upset her. The instant she found a way to leave, she'd be gone. Nothing I said or did was likely going to change her mind.

I assumed when Jack left that he'd returned to his cabin. I continued my work on the sword until I was at a good stopping point. Although I was unsure it would do any good, I decided to seek out Josie. With my thoughts weighing me down, I removed my work gear and went inside to retrieve my coat before heading out in the weather toward the lodge. To my surprise, when I came into my kitchen with Hobo at my heels, I found Jack peeking inside my cupboard.

"You ready for lunch yet?" he asked when he saw me.

"No. I'm heading over to talk to Josie."

Right away, Jack grinned from ear to ear. "That's a great idea. Go get your woman and don't take no for an answer."

I left Jack behind, knowing he'd make himself at home in my cabin. The snow had let up, and there was less than a foot on the ground. Within a few weeks there would be snow high enough to reach the kitchen window.

The front door of the lodge was unlocked. I found Josie sitting in one of the big chairs, wearing a thick coat, looking forlorn and lost, with her arms wrapped around herself. She glanced up when I stepped inside. I saw that there wasn't a fire in the fireplace and knew she must be cold.

Sensing her distress, Hobo idled over and sat down next to her.

Her sad eyes met mine briefly, and I couldn't do anything more than stare back at her. A burst of wind outside distracted me enough to cause me to look away. With little more than a slight nod of acknowledgment from Josie, I walked over to the massive fireplace, knelt, and reached for the kindling to start a fire. In a few minutes the flames licked against the twigs, and soon I was able to stack in a few logs. "Shouldn't be long before it's warm in here," I said, as a means of breaking the ice.

Her shoulders slumped forward. "Thank you."

I got up from my knees and sat in the chair opposite from her, crossing my forearms and resting them against my legs. I wasn't sure where to start.

"I shouldn't have blamed you for my mistake," she said, looking utterly miserable. Her hand absently stroked Hobo's thick fur.

"I get it, you were upset."

She gave a half laugh. "That's putting it mildly."

Seeing her this depressed was difficult. Her hair fell over her cheeks, and her eyes were downcast. "You find someone to get you out of here?" I asked, knowing it wouldn't be a problem easily solved.

Leaning back in her chair, she released a sigh. "Not really. No way is the ferry willing to return, and the price of hiring a seaplane is ridiculous. I considered going by land, you know, hiring a dog sled to come and collect me, but convincing someone to agree to that is highly unlikely." She glanced up, and a bit of hope showed in her eyes. "Don't suppose I could drive out of here?"

She knew the answer as well as I did. "The roads here are all dead ends, you know that."

"What about mail delivery? Couldn't I leave with whoever flew in the mail? Surely there's mail delivery during the winter months?"

I hesitated, knowing she wouldn't like my answer.

"I've got a post office box in Fairbanks. With so few of us remaining in Ponder, the government cuts the mail service during the winter. My sister checks it for me every few weeks. Don't really get that much, other than flyers and such. Anyone who wants to reach me knows to contact me through the Internet."

Josie sighed, the weight of the world holding her down, heavy on her shoulders.

"You spoke to your mom and explained what happened?"

"Yeah, we had a lengthy conversation."

"What about that fancy chef?" I knew that had to be a big concern for Josie. She'd been excited about her new career. I really hated the thought of her being robbed of this chance, despite my desire for her to stay.

"Chef Anton," she murmured wistfully.

"Is being stuck here going to ruin that for you?"

Her lower lip trembled, but she held it together. "I've sent him an email and I'm waiting to hear back. I want to believe he'll hold the job for me, but I don't know. Can't say I'd blame him if he hired someone else."

"I'm sorry. I really am. I know how important this opportunity is to you."

"I was the one who blew it," she said, sighing again, looking more pitiful than she had earlier, which was saying something.

Seeing Josie so down in the dumps had a strange effect on me. It took all the self-control I could muster not to take her in my arms and comfort her. The only way I could resist was to look away. I concentrated instead on the fireplace.

After a few awkward seconds, I asked, "Were you able to reach either of the Brewsters?"

Josie nodded. "They had just gotten off the ferry. Marianne felt dreadful that she'd left me behind after I told her what happened, but I have no one to blame but myself. Jerry told all of us to bring our luggage to the lobby before we went to bed. My mind was racing from our conversation, and I forgot to do it before I climbed into bed. Once I was in bed and remembered that I had to put them in the lobby, I didn't want to get dressed again. I decided I'd get up early and handle it in the morning. I guess I was thinking a few hours wouldn't matter."

"It sounds to me like a comedy of errors," I said.

"Except no one is laughing, especially not me."

That wasn't exactly true. Jack had been downright gleeful to learn that Josie was now trapped in Ponder.

"Marianne assured me I could stay at the lodge for as long as needed. That's one thing I'm grateful for. I don't know what I would have done if the Brewsters said I'd have to leave."

There wouldn't be a problem with supplies, I thought to myself. The freezer at the lodge was full of meat and vegetables and everything in between. Learning to do without fresh fruit and other produce would take some adjusting for Josie. Life in the frozen north made that a necessity. She'd find a way to manage, but that would mean keeping the fireplace going and stocked with wood, as it would be her only source of heat.

"I'm sorry for all this, Josie."

She looked up and caught my gaze, her own eyes narrowing. "Are you really sorry, Palmer? I would think having me trapped in town must look like a gift to you."

"Not against your will, it isn't." I meant that, whether Josie believed me or not. Jack might not share my opinion, but that was on him. For my part, I proposed, although badly, and Josie had said she wasn't interested.

End of story.

If she thought I was going to beg her to stay, then she was wrong. I had my answer. It wasn't the response I'd wanted, but it was one I had to accept.

Josie didn't appear to believe me.

It was time to explain why I'd come to the lodge. "I actually might have a solution for getting you back to Seattle."

It took a bit for my words to sink in. At first it seemed like Josie wasn't sure I was sincere. Then her eyes rounded with excitement. "What do you mean? Do you know someone willing to come for me?"

"I might. A friend of mine, Sawyer O'Halloran, is a bush pilot and owns a ski-plane. He has reason to fly this way every so often—"

"Define *often*," she blurted out, interrupting me.

"He's in the area every few weeks or so on business. I can reach out and ask him when he might be able to make a stop here."

"You'd do that?"

"I said I would." It was a kick in the gut to see how excited Josie got. I didn't need anything more to confirm how eager she was to leave Ponder.

To leave me.

"Once I hear back from him, I'll let you know."

"I appreciate this more than I can say."

"No problem, but I'm not making any promises."

"Of course."

As much as I wanted Josie in Ponder, I couldn't, wouldn't, manipulate events so she'd be forced to stay. I appreciated her talents as a chef—her passion, her drive, her creativity. After all, she was an artist like myself.

Some of the eagerness drained from her eyes as another thought came to her. "What do you think he'll charge me?"

Uncertain, I wasn't sure what to tell her. "Can't say, but I've never known Sawyer to be unreasonable. And as he's already going to be in the area, I strongly suspect it will be a fraction of the estimate you got earlier."

It looked as if Josie was about to cry. The one thing I couldn't deal with was a crying woman. My first impulse was to hug her, although I didn't know if she'd appreciate my touch.

"Thank you," she whispered.

"Think nothing of it," I said, and started toward the door. It was time I returned to work and kicked Jack out of my cabin before he consumed all my winter supplies.

"Can I give you a hug?" Josie asked. Before I could answer, she had crossed the room. I'd give anything to have her in my arms. But holding Josie, feeling her softness, breathing in the wonderful scent of her hair, would be pure torture now.

I didn't have a choice. She slipped her arms around my middle and pressed the side of her face against my chest.

"I don't understand why you're helping me," she said softly, as I continued to hold her close, savoring every moment. I wanted to store up this warm sensation and cling to it for as long as my memory would allow.

"I would think the answer is obvious."

Breaking away, she looked up, and her eyes locked with mine.

"I love you, Josie. I would do almost anything I could for you."

CHAPTER FIVE

Josie

I refused to unpack my suitcase. My desperate hope was that Palmer's friend would find an excuse to fly into Ponder sooner rather than later. When he arrived, I intended to be ready. For three days I lived out of my luggage, until I couldn't bear digging through my clothes another minute. I carefully set out a few items and placed them inside my drawers.

Since that first morning when I'd missed the last ferry out of Ponder, I'd avoided Palmer, which was much harder than I thought it would be. He'd stopped by the lodge any number of times and I'd found an excuse to send him on his way. I could tell he was disappointed, and after the second day of attempts, he hadn't stopped by again. I couldn't blame him. Only now, I was lonely and depressed. I was afraid if I spent time with Palmer, I would never find the courage to leave. I couldn't allow my heart to make a life-changing decision for me. This was a serious turning point in my life. I couldn't marry Palmer any more than I could live in Ponder.

With little to do at the lodge, I had nothing but time on my hands. I worked at creating recipes and menus and emailed those to Chef Anton, who had agreed to hold my position. I read two books in three days, cooked, and baked. I worked on a needlepoint project I'd brought with me that I'd started while in high school. After three full days of isolating myself and avoiding Palmer, I'd had enough. I was only hurting myself. Palmer was good company and I missed him, missed our times together. I missed Hobo, too. The husky had made his way to the lodge on his own that morning, and I nearly cried when I saw him, so thankful for the company.

Jack stopped by two or three times a day, always around mealtimes. No surprise there. If I let him, the older man would become my constant companion. He talked nonstop, suggesting meals I might consider cooking for him. He'd gone so far as to say I should thank him for giving me something to do while I waited: feed him. Just this morning, he'd brought me a package of frozen caribou meat and asked me to make his favorite stew. Because he'd generously provided the necessary ingredients, I set about putting everything together in a large Dutch oven.

"You baking bread today?" he asked, sitting on a stool inside the lodge kitchen while I browned the meat and sautéed the onions for his dinner.

"I baked bread yesterday," I reminded him.

"It's gone."

"Two loaves?" The man ate more than anyone I'd ever known.

"I gave one loaf to Palmer," he told me. "He was glad to get it, too."

I busied myself taking the meat out of the cast-iron skillet and placing it inside the pot. "Speaking of Palmer," I said, afraid to show too much interest, "how is he?"

"Busy. He's got this commission for a sword and he's working all kind of hours. Guess he wants it finished before Christmas. Mostly he's using it as a distraction, you being so close by and all."

"Oh."

"Been grumpy, too, especially when I mentioned you. You might want to bake him one of those special cobblers you make with those berries you two picked last summer. That might sweeten him up some."

My berry cobbler was Jack's favorite. He wasn't fooling me. Anything I baked for Palmer, Jack was sure to get part of. I ignored the suggestion.

"What about meals? He's eating, isn't he?"

Jack shrugged. "I don't rightly know. I suppose."

That didn't sound encouraging. "Maybe you should share part of this stew with him, seeing that there's plenty."

Jack nodded enthusiastically. "That's a great idea."

"Wonderful. I'll put everything together for you to take to him." My pride wouldn't allow me to deliver the meal, although by all that was right, I should. I hoped Palmer would see this tasty stew as a peace offering. I owed him an apology of some sort. I'd sort of backed myself into a corner and regretted it, and now I wasn't sure how to smooth the waters.

"You want *me* to take dinner to Palmer?" Jack returned indignantly. "This is your idea. You take it to him."

Part of me wanted to object, but I couldn't. Ever since Palmer said he was in love with me, I'd been struggling. Late at night I'd lay awake, thinking about marrying him and all that it would mean. I was tempted by his proposal. Really tempted. I was hounded by questions, and frankly, the answers frightened me.

Or maybe it was more the fact that his marriage proposal hadn't sounded like one. Originally, I hadn't been able to figure out what on earth he was talking about. I thought he had a case of the flu. Palmer had been talking for a good ten minutes before I had the slightest hint of where the conversation was heading. Then he'd declared his love and asked me to be his wife and all I could see were obstacles instead of the possibilities. For the last three days, I struggled. In my eagerness to work with Chef Anton, to get to my mom and to my friends, I'd discounted my feelings for Palmer, not allowing myself to admit I was in love with him. Why, oh why, did life have to be so complicated?

I'd accepted early on that a long-term relationship with him would be problematic. Repeatedly I'd told myself that once I was back in Seattle, I'd be able to forget him. Now I wasn't so sure I could make that happen. When it came to his marriage proposal, I'd been reluctant and foolish. In retrospect, I wondered what would have happened if I *had* caught the last boat out of Ponder. I was afraid once I had returned home he'd be in my heart even more than he was already, and I wasn't prepared to deal with those emotions.

"You're thinking about Palmer, aren't you?" Jack questioned, breaking into my thoughts as I stood in front of the stove, working on dinner.

"I'm sorry, I didn't hear that," I said, embarrassed to get caught.

Jack's telling eyes sparked with glee. "Palmer. He's on your mind, isn't he?"

"No," I denied. "Maybe."

Jack chuckled. "Just as I thought. Out of sight, out of mind. How's that working for you?"

I hated that he could read me that easily. I had the feeling that if my father was alive, he'd be saying the same thing to me.

"I see you don't have an answer. You know what I think?" Jack said, growing serious.

Leaving the stove area, I tried to look busy around the kitchen, cleaning out the sink. "I bet I can guess."

"I think," he said, rubbing his beard in that thoughtful way of his, "that subconsciously you wanted to miss that boat."

"What?" I flared, outraged at the suggestion. "That's ridiculous." I refused to even consider that that was the case. It wasn't even worthy of a discussion.

Jack smiled as though he held a winning lottery ticket in his hand. "Admit it, you're in love with Palmer."

Whirling around, I stared at Jack, ready to deny it, when I realized I couldn't. My shoulders sagged in defeat.

While I wasn't willing to openly admit how I felt, I decided not to say anything.

"You're confused, Josie," Jack said kindly, gently. "Can't say I blame you. Life this close to the tundra isn't easy. It can get lonely here, especially for a woman. Heard it said once that women need one another for emotional support and that kind of thing."

"Oh, so when did you become an expert on women?" I asked, grateful to turn the subject away from my feelings for Palmer.

"I don't know much about what women need," he openly admitted. "It was Angie who told me that."

"Angie Wilkerson?" I'd met her while working at the lodge. Angie and Steve—they had a cabin in Ponder. We'd exchanged greetings a few times after she won the chili cook-off, so I knew who she was. "Angie's here for the winter? In Ponder?"

"Sure is. She stays each winter, along with Steve and their two boys."

This was news to me.

"Like Palmer, Steve isn't much for city life. He works for one of those big oil companies: troubleshoots any problems that might come up with the oil line."

A sudden thought raced through my mind at the speed of light. If there were problems with the pipeline, that meant Steve might need to get out of Ponder. If he had to leave anytime soon, I might be able to catch a ride with him. Hope sprang eternal. I now had a plan B.

"Jack, if there's trouble with the pipeline, Steve has to fly out, right? I mean, he has to go to the site for repairs, doesn't he?" My mind was in a whirl, not that I wished trouble on the pipeline, but this could well develop into the escape plan I was desperately looking for.

"Nope."

"What do you mean by 'nope'?" I asked. "You just said—"

"Everything is done by computer these days, Josie. Steve can manage everything he needs to do from the comfort of his own home."

My hopes did a nosedive. "Oh."

"Angie was surprised to hear you'd missed the boat. She said she'd love to visit with you, if you'd like."

I washed my hands and dried them on the towel that was attached to my white apron. I'd call her and make a point of stopping by. I needed a friend, especially now.

"Think about what I said. I really believe your sub-conscious was at work, Josie. Given the chance, you could learn to love married life here in Ponder," Jack insisted, smiling as though he had some deeply held secret I wasn't allowed to know yet.

"Jack, please. Despite what you might think, my being stuck here wasn't intentional."

He grinned with a certain confidence that declared he was right. "So you say."

"So I know," I returned.

His smug look stayed firmly in place, and while it perturbed me, I wasn't going to waste the energy to argue further. Jack was stubborn to a fault, and I could tell it was a losing battle. Jack would never admit to being wrong.

I'd finished the dinner dishes and Jack left to return to his own cabin. I stared at the foil-covered bowl by the stove. If I was going to deliver this to Palmer, I needed to do it soon.

The one thing that shocked me about Alaska was how early it grew dark in the fall and winter. It was late in October and it was completely dark by five-thirty that afternoon. With a flashlight in hand, I dressed warmly and headed out of the lodge to Palmer's cabin. I'd traveled this path dozens of times and had no trouble finding my way.

Although it was well past the dinner hour, I noticed the lights were on in Palmer's workshop. I stood in front of the door and hesitated, gathering my nerve, unsure of my welcome. With my heart in my throat, I knocked and waited for a response.

No more than a few seconds later, the door opened. Palmer's eyes widened, as he was apparently shocked to see me.

"I brought you dinner," I said, holding out the bowl. He didn't invite me in, and with a sick feeling in the pit of my stomach, I handed it to him and turned away.

"I heard from Sawyer," he said, stopping me in my tracks. That was the friend he'd mentioned, the bush pilot who owned the ski-plane.

"You did?" I couldn't hide my excitement.

"Come inside," he said, opening the door wider. "I was just about to call it a night." He led the way from the workshop to the house, turning off the lights and heading into the kitchen with Hobo tagging behind him.

Palmer set the bowl down on the counter and washed up before turning around to face me. "I intended to have Jack give you the news earlier, but I wanted to do it myself."

He smiled, and it was as if all was forgiven and forgotten. I released a silent sigh of relief.

"Is Sawyer coming this way anytime soon?" I asked, trying not to reveal my enthusiasm. He frowned, and I knew my reaction had disappointed him.

"I figured you'd be eager to leave. Sawyer said he'd be in the area in another ten days. You can last that long, right?"

"Of course." Not that I had a choice. "Did he say anything about what he'd charge me for the flight?" This was a major concern.

"He did."

Nervous now, I moved to the opposite end of the counter, across from Palmer. He had two stools there, and I pulled one out and sat down, fearing the cost would be far beyond what I could afford and that my knees would buckle under me. The other quote I'd been given had shocked me speechless.

Palmer opened a drawer and removed a spoon before he mentioned the fee.

I gasped. I couldn't help it.

Palmer's head shot up. "Is that too much?"

"No . . . It's far less than what I expected." I was grateful and resisted the urge to leap up and hug Palmer. In only a matter of days I would be able to return to Seattle, to my mom, and to the start of my new career.

To the life I wanted, I reminded myself.

Instead of eating, Palmer placed his hands in his back pockets so that his elbows jutted out from his sides.

"What did you find out about your job with Chef Allen?"

"Chef Anton," I corrected.

"Right. Chef Anton."

"He will keep the position for me as long as I get back within the next two weeks." That was the one bright spot in my predicament.

"I checked him out on the Internet," Palmer casually mentioned. "He's young."

"Not that young. Thirty-five, I think."

Palmer snickered. "That's young. The article said he's one of the most eligible bachelors in Seattle."

I struggled to hide my amusement at Palmer's observation.

"Obviously you've met him."

"I have. A couple times." While I was impressed with his culinary skill, I'd found him arrogant and demanding, to the extreme. There'd been rumors of him abusing drugs and alcohol, but I saw no evidence of that. He was difficult, but I could deal with that. As an intern, I'd worked under a few chefs with the same overbearing attitude, and I'd managed the strong personalities while still doing my job well. That ability had gotten me the recommendation from my instructors, and the subsequent interview with Chef Anton.

"I see," Palmer said, with some reluctance.

"I believe I'll learn a great deal working under him," I offered.

"That's what I'm afraid of," Palmer muttered under his breath.

I heard him and wondered if he would repeat that. "Did you say something?"

"Not really," he said. "I'm happy he's holding the job for you, Josie."

"Thank you."

The conversation faded and there wasn't any reason for me to linger. I headed toward the door. "I guess I'd better get back to the lodge."

Palmer set aside the bowl of stew I'd delivered. "Hobo and I will walk you back."

"You don't need to do that." I'd made the trek on my own and wouldn't have a problem returning the same way.

"But I want to."

I didn't feel I could argue, and the truth was I welcomed his company.

Palmer reached for his coat and a larger flashlight than my own. We walked side by side through the dense darkness. The night was clear. I didn't think I'd ever grow accustomed to seeing as many stars as I had in Alaska.

The sky was filled with a multitude of tiny sparkling lights. Starlights. It reminded me of when I was growing up, collecting fireflies in a mason jar with my cousins on a camping trip. I'd loved camping. It was partly because of those trips with my aunt, uncle, and cousins that I applied for the position in Alaska.

We reached the lodge, and Palmer walked up the porch steps with me. I was about to thank him and open the door when he reached for my shoulders and turned me around to face him. For a long time, all we did was stare at each other. I stopped breathing at the look I saw in his eyes, the warmth, genuine care, and love.

I wasn't sure who moved first, Palmer or me. Before I realized what was happening, I was in his embrace, my arms around his neck. We were kissing as if I was sending him off to war. The heat, the need, and the passion were deeper than anything we'd shared to this point.

By the time we broke apart we were both panting like we'd been held underwater too long. I placed my hand over my heart and took a step back. I looked at Palmer, and he seemed to be as much in a daze as I was.

"Wow," I whispered, unsure of what had just happened. Not that I regretted it.

Palmer started down the steps.

"Palmer," I called out.

At the bottom of the steps he turned to face me.

"What was that kiss all about?" I asked, wanting him to clarify it, because I certainly couldn't.

"Not sure," he said, with a pragmatic tone. "Guess I wanted you to remember me when you met Chef Allen."

"Anton."

"Whatever," he muttered, as he returned to his cabin.

CHAPTER SIX

Josie

I spent a sleepless night, unable to stop thinking about Palmer. I loved the way he kissed. His kisses were addictive. I knew that once I returned home, I'd have trouble forgetting him and our time in Ponder. Tossing and turning, I was forced to answer the question: Did I *want* to forget him? My heart sank when I realized that I didn't. Palmer was a part of me now, but that didn't alter my circumstances or my obligations.

No matter how I felt about him, I needed to get back to Seattle. I'd made a commitment to Chef Anton. I had worked hard for this wonderful opportunity—darn hard. It made no sense to give it all up to live in a town where my training, my love of food, and my talent would basically be wasted. Oh sure, I could continue to cook for the lodge six months out of the year. But I knew myself well enough to realize that it would soon bore me. Earlier, I'd tried talking to my mother, who seemed distracted and wasn't much help. All she would tell me was to follow my heart. But my heart wasn't leading the way, unlike my brain, which continued to spin most of the night, unable to provide viable solutions.

I woke groggy and cranky, unfairly irritated at Palmer for the terrible quandary I faced. This was all his fault. I wish I could've talked to Jack about my feelings. But as much as I liked and trusted him, Jack was biased. He wouldn't hesitate to tell me to marry Palmer. Before I'd messed everything up by missing the boat, I'd hoped that once I was back in Seattle where I belonged, I'd gain perspective about my time in Ponder and my feelings for Palmer. This delay had complicated everything.

Disgruntled, my mind repeatedly reviewed my limited options as I dressed and sipped my morning coffee. Out of the blue I remembered Jack's ludicrous suggestion that I had intentionally missed the boat. Just thinking about Jack's theory irritated me. I'd had every intention of being on board that ferry when it pulled away from the dock.

Like Palmer said, it was a comedy of errors. No one

was to blame, and at the same time we all were. Palmer for the last-minute proposal. Marianne Brewster for assuming I had changed my mind. And, of course, me for setting the wrong time on my alarm and neglecting to take my luggage to the lobby.

Something else Jack said came to mind as well. He'd mentioned that Angie Wilkerson wintered in Ponder and she'd invited me to stop by that afternoon. Talking with another woman, I decided, was exactly what I needed. I waited until mid-morning, bundled up in my warmest clothes, and headed out to her cabin, following the tracks made by a snowmobile.

During the brisk ten-minute walk, I had to pass through the middle of Ponder. Past the one tavern with the Baptist church right next door. Past the all-service hardware store on the other side of the street, now closed for the winter. Inside the store was anything and everything a person could possibly need, including a pharmacy, a liquor store, a post office, and what passed for a bank. The Terry family had run it for years in-season, and they spent their winters with their oldest daughter in Texas. In the spring they would return about the same time that the Brewsters opened the lodge.

Next to the hardware store was the second tavern in town, by the Free Methodist Church. Pastor Gene was a retired minister who served during the busy season, then left early in October. I'd enjoyed his sermons and the man himself. He stopped by the lodge for dinners every Sunday, compliments of the Brewsters. It was at this church that I'd first met Angie and Steve. During the tourist season, a priest flew in for a Saturday-evening Mass once a month.

There was a lending library in town, too, for locals and visitors. Lilly Appleton willingly lent books to anyone who wanted to read them, right out of her home. Her entire living room was filled with bookshelves. It'd only been in the last couple years that she'd gone to Fairbanks for the winters, since she was getting older and was a widow now. She'd left town on that last ferry, too.

I continued walking, the cold biting my face, until I reached the Wilkersons' place. Angie opened the door when I knocked and greeted me with a huge smile.

"Come on in," she said, taking me by the arm and leading me inside, where it was warm.

It took me a few minutes to take off all my layers. By the time I finished, Angie had a pot of tea steeping on the table. She was a tall, thinnish woman with long, dark hair in a thick braid that reached to the middle of her back. Two little boys, about four and five years old, sat on the floor with Legos scattered around them. They appeared to be building a skyscraper. Intent on their task, they barely noticed me.

"I was surprised when I heard you'd missed the ferry," Angie said. "You must have been frantic."

"I was, but Palmer knows someone who can fly me into Fairbanks in a few days."

Angie glanced up from pouring tea. "Sawyer O'Halloran?"

"You know him?"

"Everyone close to the Arctic knows Sawyer. So Palmer did it, then," she said, with an incredulous tone. "He arranged a way for you to leave?"

I wasn't sure I understood her shock. "That surprises you?"

"It does. He's crazy about you."

Already the conversation had turned uncomfortable. "Yes, well, I . . . My life is in Seattle." I didn't mention I had a dream job waiting or explain that this was an opportunity other culinary graduates envied. Any one of my fellow classmates would have given just about anything to work with Chef Anton.

Angie sighed. "I'll admit your decision to leave is a disappointment, but I'm being selfish. I'd love it if you stayed. So few women live here, especially during the winter season."

"It shocked me to hear that you stay behind. Isn't

it hard on you?" All I could think about was the loneliness Angie must feel, the lack of amenities and other services.

The other woman lifted the mug and rested her elbows on the oak tabletop. "It is and it isn't. I miss everyone who leaves after the season, but there's real beauty here during the winter months. I didn't appreciate it in the beginning, but I do now."

Seeing the stars and the Northern Lights with Palmer and Hobo immediately flooded my mind. We'd seen them several times; crazy as it sounded, we *heard* them, too. They made a crackling sound. And just this morning, I'd watched an Arctic fox frolic in the snow. The stunted fir trees, with their limbs weighed down by the heavy snow, looked like a Christmas-card scene. The beauty was everywhere. I'd tried to ignore it, but I couldn't. I had to agree with Angie.

"Doesn't the isolation bother you?" I asked, after taking a sip of my tea. It was a lovely blend of orange and spice that I recognized as one of my favorites from Seattle.

"It did in the beginning, before Mason and Oliver arrived."

I looked over at the two boys and smiled, surprised that they were so easily entertained. The stack of Legos had reached the height of Oliver, who had stood up, adding pieces until the pile leaned precariously to the left. He giggled, delighted when the bricks broke apart and scattered across the floor.

"Mason, help your brother put the Legos back in the box," Angie told her older son.

Mason reached for the plastic tub and dragged it over to where Oliver now sat. "Can I have a cookie?"

"After the two of you pick up."

Watching the exchange gave me time to collect my thoughts. "How did you and Steve meet?" I asked, curious now. Jack had mentioned that Angie's husband wasn't much of a city man. Palmer wasn't either. I knew he and Steve were friends, but little else.

"We met in Fairbanks," Angie said, keeping an eye on the youngsters. "I had a summer job working in the fishing industry outside of Anchorage. The money was great, and I needed it to supplement my scholarship. A friend and I decided at the close of the fishing season that we wanted to travel past the Arctic Circle, so we took the train from Anchorage, through Denali, to Fairbanks, where we would be able to hire a bush pilot."

"That was when you met Steve?"

"Yes. I was at the airfield, talking to one of the pilots,

inquiring how much it would be to fly to Bettles. I'd read about this small town and found a lodge there and booked it for one night."

"No road into Bettles, right?"

"None."

It was the same here in Ponder, although the town was below the Arctic Circle.

"Steve was at the airfield also, looking to find a pilot to take him back to Ponder, when he overheard our conversation. We got to talking and he invited me out to dinner that night and I accepted. We both had flights out the following morning: me to Bettles and Steve to Ponder. My friend had taken a liking to the bush pilot, so she had her own date." She paused long enough to take another sip of tea. "Steve and I had dinner, and I guess you could say we hit it off. We talked until the restaurant closed. Up to that point, I'd dated quite a bit, but I'd never met anyone as interesting and likable as Steve. We clicked. I don't know how else to say it."

"How did you make it work?" I asked. I didn't mean to be intrusive, but I was genuinely interested.

"After our dinner, I canceled my trip to Bettles, and Steve canceled his flight back to Ponder. We were together every minute in Fairbanks until it was time for me to return to Oregon, three days later. I hated to leave, and Steve hated for me to go, but I had to get back for school."

"You two must have kept in touch, then."

Angie nodded. "We talked every day for months."

Mason tugged at her sleeve, with Oliver right by his side. "We're done, Mommy. Can we have our cookies now?"

"Yes, good job, boys!" Angie leaned forward and kissed the tops of their heads before standing and reaching into the apple-shaped jar on the counter. She handed each of her sons a homemade cookie. They raced out of the kitchen and toward the family room.

"I'm going to read to Oliver now," Mason shouted back to his mom.

Angie smiled. "Mason has memorized all the words to his favorite books. He's starting to read on his own. Amazing how smart he is. Oliver, too."

I watched the two boys and I felt my heart constrict. I hoped for a family of my own one day.

"Okay," Angie said, sighing. "Back to our story. I returned to college. It was my last year and I had everything all set in my mind on how I wanted my life to go. Marrying Steve and moving to Ponder weren't part of the plan."

I could relate to that. "What changed your mind?" I asked.

"Not what. Who. It was Steve. I'd never met anyone like him. He was independent, strong, and capable. I thought about him constantly. Like I said, we talked every day. My grades started to drop. My parents were worried. They were afraid I wasn't going to graduate. I spent so much of my time focused on Steve, despite the distance between us, that my studies suffered."

"But you did graduate, didn't you?"

"Mom and Dad had every reason to be concerned that I wouldn't be able to pull it off and get my diploma. I let everything slide, living between phone calls and emails from Steve. My emotions were all over during that time: One day I'd be elated, and the next I'd be in the dumps. But yes, in the end I did manage to graduate. Steve promised to fly down for my graduation, and he did. He came with an engagement ring. Before he proposed, he talked to my parents about marrying me."

As she spoke, a faraway look came over Angie. "I hadn't seen him since the day I'd left Fairbanks. I wasn't sure how I'd feel when we saw each other again, but you know what's crazy?"

I could only speculate.

"It was like no time had gone by at all. The minute I saw him again, I knew this was the man I was going to love for the rest of my life."

"But . . ." I tried to interject.

"I know what you're going to say, because my mom said the very same thing. She thought I was crazy: that I'd be wasting my education, stuck up here in this desolate town in Alaska."

Admittedly, these were my thoughts, too. Angie had spent four years to get her college degree, only to marry Steve and move to Ponder? No wonder her family had been concerned.

"What was your major?" I asked, rather than tell her what I really thought.

"English literature. Everyone assumed that upon graduation, I'd go on to teach. To be fair, that had been my original intention. I love the written word and wanted to share my enthusiasm with young minds."

"There's no school here, is there?"

"Mason is halfway through his kindergarten curriculum already, and Oliver is in preschool. I homeschool them. It's online, like most everything else in this neck of the woods."

Because my days working at the lodge had been full of my duties there, I hadn't had the opportunity to get to know Angie other than in passing. I was full of questions and fascinated about her life in Ponder.

"So how are you using your education?" I asked.

She smiled, having anticipated this question. "I've been writing novels under my maiden name, Angela Wellington."

The name sounded familiar to me, until it hit me. "Angela *Wellington*?" I repeated softly. My eyes rounded. "I *know* you! You write historical fiction. I've read two of your books." I was stunned. Speechless. My mouth must have been hanging open, because Angie burst out laughing.

"The thing is, I would never have considered a writing career if I wasn't married to Steve and living in Ponder."

I had no idea that I'd been living in the same town as renowned author Angela Wellington. "How did you even get started writing?" I asked.

"It just happened. I read a lot the first winter that Steve and I spent in Ponder, and was inspired by a book I'd read, wishing there was a sequel to it. Steve was the one who suggested I write my own story, which I did while I was pregnant with Mason. I don't think anyone was more surprised than I was when a publisher accepted my manuscript. It usually doesn't happen that way. A lot of writers submit manuscripts for years before they ever sell one, but my first manuscript was accepted. A writing friend of mine told me that it wasn't fair—I hadn't suffered enough!"

I laughed.

"I've written three books in the last four years and am working on my fourth now. It's harder to get in writing time as the boys have become more active, so I write during their naps and early in the morning before they're awake. My days, though, are theirs. My husband and sons are my focus."

The few times I'd met Angie, I'd liked her. That feeling grew stronger as we talked over the pot of tea. "I had no idea you were an author."

"I don't advertise it. I love being a writer and storyteller." She looked away for a second before making eye contact with me. "I would love it if you and Palmer got together. I've never seen him happier than he has been these last six months since you arrived. He's a different person."

"I don't think I could make a life here, Angie," I confessed. "I've always lived in Seattle and there's so little here in Ponder."

"There's Palmer," she reminded me. "You love him, don't you?"

I couldn't deny it. "I do, but I have a job waiting for me. I signed a contract."

"Then go. I did. I finished school. You need this time away, and Palmer does, too. If what you have is real, you'll know in time. This isn't a decision you need to make this minute. It won't hurt to put some distance between the two of you for a while."

Angie was the voice of reason. While I had an important decision to make, she was right—it didn't require an overnight answer. Palmer had accepted that I was leaving and, in fact, had helped me find a way to get to Seattle. He understood that I needed to do this. I was the one who was putting pressure on myself.

It made sense. Once I was home and settled in to my job, I'd have a better understanding of what was best for both Palmer and me. Still, one problem concerned me. From the earliest time I could remember, all I'd ever wanted to do was become a chef. I'd worked long and hard to get this far. I wasn't sure I could give up everything I'd hoped to achieve. I wasn't sure I could find a way to use my talents in Ponder, like Angie had. There were no book deals for me, and no exciting career opportunities were going to present themselves to me here.

*

The rest of the morning sped past. It seemed like we'd been chatting only a few minutes when I realized it was time for lunch, and Angie mentioned she had to put the boys down for their naps soon. I hugged her good-bye and started back to the lodge.

Jack found me on the return trip. "I see you were at Angie's place," he said, coming to walk alongside me.

"We had a great visit."

I was about to thank him for getting the two of us together when he interrupted.

"What's for lunch?"

"There's plenty of caribou stew left," I reminded him. "I froze it for you to enjoy after I'd left. And I really shouldn't be using the Brewsters' kitchen to be cooking for you."

"I agree," he said, surprising me. "Think you should come to my cabin to cook, then. You gotta eat. I gotta eat. I'll gladly give you whatever provisions you need in exchange for a home-cooked meal."

I eyed him suspiciously, unsure what the state of his kitchen might be.

"What's the problem?" he grumbled. "It sounds like a fair enough deal to me."

"Show me your kitchen first."

"Sure. No problem. I was thinking elk spaghetti for

tonight." Jack hunted wild game and his freezer was full of it, along with salmon, halibut, and other treasures from the Alaskan waters.

I sighed. "You ever heard of plain old beef?"

"Sure, I've heard of beef, just never seen a cow in the wilderness of Alaska. Would gladly eat one if I did. You coming or not?"

I nodded my head. There was no debating with the man.

After following Jack to his cabin, I was pleasantly surprised to find it clean and his kitchen well supplied and organized.

"Why do you look so shocked?" he asked.

"I can't imagine," I joked, and rolled up my sleeves.

Cooking for a man who appreciated his food was a pleasure, I had to admit, and the two of us had a wonderful evening. I was going to miss this, and so much more.

CHAPTER SEVEN

Palmer

The steel blade I'd so carefully crafted had developed a crack. I groaned when I saw it, sick that I'd spent weeks working on this replica Civil War sword, polishing it to a fine sheen. Now I would be forced to start from the beginning. I threw back my head and groaned. I'd wanted to finish this project well before Christmas, but now that would be pushing it.

If I had anyone to blame, the fault would fall squarely on Josie's shoulders. She occupied far too much of my thoughts. I'd made the mistake of checking out the great Chef Anton online, and now I was riddled with doubts. The guy had it all. He was successful, and his restaurants were highly touted. I had to assume he was wealthy, and to top everything off, he was single and good-looking.

I wanted to dislike the man, which was unfair and unlike me. My overriding fear was that Josie would fall for him. They'd be working closely together day in and day out. It would be only natural that two people with shared interests and who worked side by side would fall in love. I know, it was crazy. I was insanely jealous of a man I'd never met and, frankly, one that I hoped never to meet.

For three days after Josie had missed that last ferry out of Ponder, she avoided me. For some screwy reason, she blamed me. This time apart made me realize that I had to do everything in my power to see that she made it back to Seattle. I loved her, and I wanted her to have this opportunity. What I hadn't taken into consideration was Chef Anton's role in how I was feeling. Seeing her go meant that the two of them might possibly end up together.

My gut tightened. I wasn't a man who suffered from doubts. That wasn't who I was. I knew that Josie was heading home soon, and I'd made up my mind to do the best I could to keep the lines of communication open between us. If she fell for that handsome, rich chef whom she already admired, then she wasn't the woman for me after all. In theory, my reasoning sounded good, but it didn't do anything to lessen the pain in my gut.

The one bright spot was that I'd heard from Jack that Josie and Angie had been spending time together. Steve and I were longtime friends. I remembered when he'd first met his wife and how crazy he was about Angie. They'd known each other only a few days before Angie returned for her senior year of college in Oregon. There had to be a lot of college boys interested in her. Steve had never given it a thought, at least not that he'd mentioned to me. They'd talked every day, emailed, kept in touch. I was determined to do the same—I'd make sure I wasn't ever far from her thoughts by keeping the lines of communication open. I wasn't giving up on us, not by a long shot.

Hobo interrupted me and wanted out. I could use a break as well. I grabbed my coat from the hook by the door and walked toward town, my boots crunching into the hard snow.

Hobo did his business and quickly returned to my side. As I neared town, I happened to catch a glimpse of Josie. She was outside of Steve and Angie's cabin, playing with their youngest boy, Oliver. I stood frozen in place as I watched them playing some silly kid's game in the snow. Seeing Josie with the little boy, I was mesmerized, dreaming of the day she would be playing with a child of our own. A man could hope.

She must have felt my presence because she looked in my direction and smiled. The simple action went through me like a hot spoon digging into a bowl of ice cream. Raising her hand, she gave me a small wave before Oliver hit her square in the stomach with a snowball. Throwing her head back and laughing, she took off and chased after the boy, grabbing him by the waist and twirling him around.

I don't think I could have loved her more at that moment; my heart felt like it was melting inside my chest. I didn't know how it would ever be possible for me to watch her leave, and I knew the time would fly by before I would have to do just that.

Hobo barked when he saw Oliver and Josie, and took after them. I reluctantly followed, fearing Josie would sense my vulnerability to her and the power she held over me.

Oliver dropped to his knees to play with Hobo while I joined Josie. "Hey," I said, finding my tongue thick and my speech awkward.

She beamed a brilliant smile at me, and I swear it was all I could do to refrain from pulling her toward me and kissing her senseless.

"Hey," she said.

For a few uncomfortable moments all we did was stare at each other, until she broke the ice.

"I'm cooking for Jack tonight at his place. You want to join us?"

After all the meals Jack had helped himself to at my cabin, I didn't hesitate. "Sure. What time?"

She shrugged, as if she hadn't considered that. "We'll eat when you arrive."

"Okay." Why, oh why, did she have to be *so* perfect?

"Palmer? Palmer?" Oliver jerked at the bottom of my jacket. With my full focus on Josie, I hadn't paid any attention to the four-year-old.

"Yes, Oliver?" I asked, squatting down so we were at eye level.

"Can Hobo stay and play with us?" Oliver's cheeks were red from the cold and his chubby face was round and hopeful.

I looked up at Josie. "It's all right with me," she said. "If you don't mind."

"Sure, have fun."

"You want me to bring him home once we're ready to go inside?"

Hobo knew his way to the shop on his own. I think what she was asking was if she would be interrupting me and my work when she brought him back. Not one to miss the opportunity to see her, my answer was clear.

"That would be great."

Josie gave my hand a gentle squeeze, and my heart felt like it was going to break free of my chest. This woman! How would I ever find the strength to let her go?

When Josie dropped off the dog a bit later, we spent more time kissing than talking. A full three hours passed before she left, and I returned to my workshop and to the blade I'd spent a copious amount of time designing and creating. This was by far my most prestigious commission, and it was important that I provide a product worthy of the trust placed in me. Bottom line: I would need to start all over, as there was no way to repair the crack in the blade. I was about to get started when my workshop door opened and Jack stepped inside, looking cheerful and happy. Hobo got up from his bed to greet my friend.

"I'm busy," I told him. I'd spent the better part of the afternoon with Josie and needed to get back to work.

"Saw Josie was here."

"Yup." I ignored him as best I could and built up the fire, ready to melt the steel.

"She said she invited you to dinner."

"She did." I added wood to the burner.

"At my cabin."

"She mentioned that, too."

"She's cooking."

"Know that." I dug for a fresh piece of steel in my pile.

"You gonna be there?"

"I'll be there. Listen, Jack, I really need to get back to work. We'll connect later, okay?" I looked toward the door, hoping he'd take the hint.

He buried his hands in his pockets and shuffled his feet. "You really going to let her leave?"

"I don't have a choice, Jack. It's not like I can kidnap her and force her to stay."

His eyes widened. "Maybe *you* couldn't, but *I* could."

"Jack, of all the ridiculous ideas!"

"'Course, she'd be upset for the first few days. She'd get over it, though. No need letting her know you were in on the plan. I wouldn't tie her up or anything, just keep her locked in the kitchen. She'd need her hands free to prepare meals. What do you think?"

"You're off your ever-lovin' rocker. Don't even think of doing anything that stupid. Promise me, Jack. Josie would never forgive you. I'd never forgive you. And worse yet, she'd blame me."

101

The older man's shoulders sank with defeat. "I was afraid you were going to say that."

"Promise me," I emphasized.

"Promise," he muttered, and started toward the door. "Josie said we wouldn't eat until you arrived. I like my meals early, so don't be late."

"I'll do my best," I replied, trying to hide my amusement.

And with that, Jack was gone.

I worked late into the afternoon, well past dusk, and knew Jack would be pacing with impatience by the time I decided to quit for the day. I was making progress on the sword, but I'd lost valuable time.

It'd been hours since I'd last eaten and I had to admit I was hungry. Earlier in the week, Jack had brought me a fresh loaf of sourdough bread Josie had baked, still warm, fresh from the oven. The butter had melted, soaking into the bread. It was delicious. The best. I'd devoured the entire loaf within two days. My mind imagined Josie in the kitchen, kneading the dough and then shaping it into loaves before baking it. I'd held that thought in my mind long afterward. I hoped she'd have time to bake again before she left, although I had the feeling I'd be fighting Jack for a share.

I hurriedly headed out the door. Hobo was fed, and I left him at home, although he wasn't happy about it. When I reached Jack's cabin, I knocked on the door and didn't wait for a response before I let myself in. I was greeted by the most wonderful aroma of chili.

Jack, who'd been sitting by the fireplace, immediately leapt to his feet. "It's about time," he said, exasperated. "My stomach is as hollow as an empty well. It's been torture waiting for you. Don't you ever look at your phone?"

"My phone?" I repeated.

"Jack sent you a text," Josie explained.

I arched my thick brows. "You know how to text?"

"Josie taught me, and I didn't send you just one, I sent six."

Swallowing a grin, I apologized. "I'm sorry for the delay."

"As you should be. I told you I like to eat early." Jack had already taken his place at the table and held his spoon upright, letting us know he was ready to be served.

Josie went into the kitchen and I followed. "You need any help?" I asked.

She handed me a platter of corn bread. "You can take

this to the table, but keep it away from Jack. He's eaten half the pan as it is."

That didn't come as a surprise. "Will do." I carried the plate over to the table and set it at the far end while Josie delivered a large pot of chili, which she set in the middle.

Jack bowed his head and said a shortened version of grace. "Good friends, good meat. Good God, let's eat!"

Chuckling, I reached for the corn bread before handing the plate to Josie, who asked me about the sword. Soon we were all talking and laughing together. This was the thing with Josie. She was easy to talk to, easy to be with, and even easier to love.

When the meal was finished, Josie and I washed dishes while Jack set up Yahtzee, a game he enjoyed. We played for an hour and Jack won both games. We might have stayed longer if Jack hadn't pointedly yawned, indicating that he was ready for us to go. While Josie put the game away, I grabbed my coat and then helped her into hers. After saying good night to Jack, we left together.

I offered Josie my arm and she took it as we strolled toward the lodge. For the first few minutes we were both silent, and then we started to speak at the same time.

"I wanted—"

"I'm sorry about the sword—"

"You first," I said, and gestured with my hand for her to speak.

"I was about to say how much I enjoyed spending time with you this afternoon."

Thinking about the kisses we'd shared and the books we'd discussed reminded me how empty my life would feel once she returned to Seattle. I didn't allow myself to dwell on that. "Me, too."

"It's been a good day. I especially liked getting to know Angie better."

"You mentioned that you had a nice visit with her this afternoon."

Josie nodded and looked down at her boots, appearing to have more to say. "Angie told me how she and Steve met and how they stayed in touch once she went back to college."

I knew the story well, having been friends with Steve for years.

"I'm hoping . . ." she said and paused. "What I'm trying to say is that when I go back to Seattle it doesn't need to be the end for us."

My spirits rose. "I know I don't want it to be."

She looked toward me, her face glowing in the moonlight. "You'll keep in touch?"

"Sure. Will you?" She had to do her part. This couldn't all be one-sided.

"Of course. Be patient with me, though. I'm going to have a lot of responsibilities at Chez Anton."

"The name of the restaurant is Chez Anton?"

To my surprise, Josie giggled.

"What's so funny?" I asked.

"Just now. You said Chef's name like you were sucking on a lemon. What is it with you and him? Ever since you admitted to looking him up online, you've been sort of weird about him."

She was right. I didn't realize I'd been so open in my dislike and distrust of the other man. "Yeah, well, he can offer you more than I ever could."

"All he's offering me is a *job,* Palmer. It isn't like we're romantically involved."

Not yet, you mean, I added silently to myself.

We neared the lodge and I looked at Josie. She glanced up at me, her eyes connecting with mine, the moonlight shining down on us both. For one crazed moment I was caught up in her beauty and found it impossible to breathe.

"I leave soon," she whispered.

I was happy to hear the regret in her voice. "Next Friday," I stated, already dreading the day.

Josie wrapped her arm around my mine and leaned her head against me all the way back to the lodge. We continued walking slowly until we reached the lodge steps.

"I'm going to miss you something awful," she whispered.

I thought I heard her voice crack. I was about to take her in my arms and assure her that the feelings were mutual when she broke away, hurried inside, and closed the door.

Shocked, I stood outside as large snowflakes started to fall. I would miss her, too, something awful.

CHAPTER EIGHT

Josie

In the time that followed the dinner with Jack and Palmer, I'd spent nearly every spare minute with Palmer. Because he needed to work on the commission for the sword, I left him to himself in the mornings. At noon I brought him lunch and the two of us would sit and eat together. We talked and laughed, and before I knew it half the afternoon was gone.

Although I didn't have a lot of experience with men, I'd never met anyone who made me as comfortable as Palmer did. He shared stories about his father, who had worked for a military contractor in Alaska, traveling all over the world, while the family had stayed behind in a town about a hundred miles north of Fairbanks. In addition to bringing souvenirs back for Palmer and his sister, Alicia, he'd tell them tales from his travels in Lebanon, Jordan, and Italy, to name only a few. As an adult, Palmer had been content to remain in Alaska, although he'd worked briefly in the Aleutian Islands before settling in Ponder. His parents had retired in Anchorage but continued to travel. Alicia, older than Palmer by two years, had married, started a family, and settled down in Fairbanks. From what I could tell, Palmer and his sister were close.

We spent the evenings in his cabin, each of us reading, content simply to be together. Palmer was well read, and we often discussed the books we were reading, but we didn't need lengthy conversations to communicate. If you didn't know us, you'd have thought we were an old married couple, so attuned to each other that words weren't necessary. When he walked me back to the lodge at night, he would take me in his arms and kiss me until my knees grew weak and I clung to him. Every night it was harder and harder to let him return to his cabin alone.

Deep down I knew Palmer was wishing that I'd have a change of heart and remain in Ponder. He'd never asked me again, though, and I appreciated that he didn't, because, quite frankly, I didn't know if I could refuse him a second time. Leaving Ponder loomed on the horizon, and I knew without question that I would need to go.

I was tempted to stay.

So tempted.

But I feared if I did that one day, I'd look back on my life and regret it. I would remember that decision and ask myself where my career might have taken me if I hadn't given up this opportunity. The desire to pursue my dreams outweighed the temptation.

The remaining days before Sawyer was due to arrive passed far too quickly. I'd begun crossing them off on the calendar in my room. I stared at the one blank space left before the ski-plane was scheduled to land on the now frozen lake. My suitcase was ready, my drawers empty. My flight arrangements from Fairbanks into Seattle had been rebooked. Mom was counting the hours until she could hug me again.

My own feelings were mixed. I longed to get back to Seattle with the same intensity that I desired to stay in Ponder. One minute I was convinced I couldn't leave Palmer, and the next I was equally determined to go.

For my final night, Angie and Steve invited Jack, Palmer, and me for a farewell dinner and party. My mood, as I dressed for this final evening with my friends, was anything but festive. I sniffled as I reached for my coat to walk to the Wilkersons' cabin, unsure how I was going to manage to get through the evening without breaking into tears.

When I left the lodge, I found Palmer pacing back and forth across the lodge porch, his fists bunched at his sides.

"Palmer?"

He stopped abruptly and whirled around to face me. "You ready?"

"Palmer, are you okay?"

He exhaled and slowly nodded. He didn't tell me what was eating at him, but I knew. He, too, hated the thought of me leaving come morning, but neither of us spoke of it, not wanting to make this any more difficult than it already was. He forced a grin and I struggled to hold back tears. I refused to let my emotions take over—otherwise, the entire evening would be ruined. No way was I going to get all maudlin in front of my friends.

Palmer must have read the agony in my eyes, because he brought me into his arms and hugged me, holding me close and tight like he never wanted to release me.

"It's going to be okay," he said, reluctantly letting me go.

"No, it isn't," I replied. "This is killing me, Palmer.

You made me fall in love with you, and now I'm miserable."

"We've talked about this, Josie. You'll go to Seattle, work with Chef Allen."

He grinned as he said the name, teasing me.

"And we'll figure everything out from there," he continued.

"You'll come visit?" I knew he intended to deliver the sword to the East Coast sometime in December, and that seemed the perfect time for a layover in Seattle.

He hesitated and then nodded.

Tossing my arms around his neck, I rose on the tips of my toes to kiss him. Despite my best effort to hold back my tears, I sniffled. "Thank you."

"Don't cry," he murmured, groaning. "Your tears are kryptonite."

"That's the problem. You think you're Superman."

Not wanting it to end, we begrudgingly broke apart, knowing we had to get to the party. Palmer placed his arm around my shoulders, bringing me close to his side. I leaned against him, needing his strength.

"We'd better go, or we'll be late."

The last thing I felt like doing was attending a party, especially a party celebrating me.

*

Despite my initial mood, we had a wonderful evening. Angie and Steve were gracious hosts. Angie had cooked a delicious dinner, and then games followed that included the adults and the two boys. When it was time for Mason and Oliver to go to bed, Steve carried his sons, one under each arm, up the stairs to their bedroom. Jack and Palmer tagged along because they were recruited to tell the boys a story before their lights were turned off for the night.

With the men out of the room, I helped Angie with the dinner dishes, scraping the plates before setting them in the dishwasher. "It's going to be hard to leave come morning," I commented.

Angie dried her hands on a dishtowel. "I remember Steve driving me to the airport after our first three days together. We'd known each other such a short time; I was already half in love with him. I almost missed my plane because neither one of us could find a way to say goodbye. I realize it sounds trite, but I believe things turn out the way they were meant to be."

More than anything, I wanted to believe that was true. "It's hard to go . . . hard to leave . . ."

"Trust me, I know that all too well," Angie said, reassuring me with a gentle pat on my shoulder. "I did, and it was for the best. It was months before we saw each other again. It all worked out in the end, and it will for you and Palmer, too."

"Keep an eye on Palmer for me, will you?"

"Of course."

"He works too hard and skips meals." I needed to know that someone would look after him.

"I'll make sure we have him over for dinner at least once a week."

"Jack, too?" I'd grown especially fond of the old sourdough.

I could feel the tears gathering in my eyes and blinked several times to keep them at bay.

"You want me to feed Jack?" she cried in mock horror. "That man eats more than six hungry lumberjacks."

"He does," I agreed.

"Now, stop those tears," Angie said, swiping at the moisture gathering under her eyes. "Much more of this and we'll both be sobbing."

I knew she was right, and we half laughed and half cried, unable to decide which emotion was the strongest, each of us flipping between the two. "I'll keep in touch," I promised.

"I will, too."

Angie turned back to the sink. Then, almost as if she found it necessary to share the realities of life near the tundra, she added, "If you do decide to marry Palmer, you should know that living in Ponder won't always be easy. Love will carry you only so far."

"You made the transition," I reminded her. I appreciated Angie's words of advice. I'd enjoyed the six months I'd spent in the area, but it wasn't anywhere close to being Shangri-la. It was the first time in my life I'd lived in a place where I couldn't reach a fresh market within twenty minutes, not to mention an emergency medical facility. Even the Ponder post office closed in the off-season. I'd never heard of such a thing.

"Steve asked me to give it a year," Angie explained. "He told me that at the end of that time, if I wanted to move, then he agreed that we would move to a larger town."

"You chose to stay, though."

"I did, although I was pregnant with Mason before our first anniversary. By then I'd come to love the town and the people. Could I really leave Lilly or Jack and the other friends I'd made? In the end, I realized Ponder had become my home, too."

"But you found a way to make use of your degree. There isn't that opportunity for me here," I argued. Angie could write her books in this remote place, and yes, of course, I could always cook for the lodge, but that

wasn't going to be enough for me. Not after all the sacrifices I'd made to get a culinary degree. Angie brought up
the idea about writing a food blog, but without access to
fresh ingredients year-round, it seemed out of the question. As far as I could figure, few, if any, employment
options existed for me in Ponder.

Angie and I had finished the dishes when the men
returned from putting the boys to bed. We all gathered
in front of the fireplace, and Steve brought out a bottle
of wine.

"Been saving this for a special occasion," he said and
sighed. "Guess Josie leaving tomorrow is it, although I
don't think any one of us is celebrating the fact."

Angie joined her husband and placed her arms around
him. "Actually, I have a piece of good news. It looks like
Mason and Oliver are going to be big brothers."

It took Steve a couple seconds to understand that
he was about to become a dad for the third time. When
he did, he let out a whoop of joy, grabbed Angie around
the waist, and whirled her around.

Once he released Angie, I hugged her, while Jack and
Palmer slapped Steve across the back. Steve poured wine
for us all, and Angie grabbed a glass of apple juice as
we all saluted the latest addition to the population of
Ponder, Alaska.

When the evening was over, Palmer walked me back to the lodge. We had our arms around each other the entire way, clinging to each other before it became necessary to part.

"Sawyer said he'd be landing around nine-thirty, right around sunrise."

I already knew the time and wished it wasn't so early. I wanted to delay my departure as long as possible.

"Will you walk me out to the dock in the morning?" I asked, not wanting to waste a single minute we had left.

His hesitation surprised me.

"Palmer?" I asked, when he didn't respond.

"Forgive me, Josie, but I don't know that I can."

His refusal shocked me. I understood his reluctance; I had my own. A good-bye, no matter how brief, would be difficult.

"I don't know if I have the strength to let you go," he admitted. "It might be best if we said our good-byes now."

I didn't like it, but I understood.

With his arms around me and his lips close to my neck, he said, "I need you to do one last favor for me."

"Anything." I was struggling not to cry.

"When you get back to Seattle, please don't tell me anything about Chef Allen."

"Anton."

He grinned sheepishly. "You know who I mean."

I considered his request and frowned, needing to make sure I understood what he was asking and why. "You don't want me to tell you anything about him? That's nuts. Why not?"

Palmer eased away from me and rubbed a hand down his beard. He looked utterly miserable. "He's perfect for you, and—"

"Palmer!" I couldn't believe what I was hearing.

"No, hear me out. Please. I'm already jealous that he's going to be spending all that time with you. He's everything I'm not. I realize I sound like a whiny little boy and I apologize, but for my sanity, keep that relationship with the chef entirely to yourself."

"I'm not going to be dating him, Palmer. Not ever. I know better than to mix my professional and personal life. You have nothing to worry about."

"Maybe not. Time will tell."

His request shocked me. I didn't know what he'd read about Chef Anton that made him think I'd fall for the renowned restaurant owner. I wasn't a fickle teenager, after all. And I loved *Palmer*.

"You need to trust me. First off, I'm not the least bit attracted to him, and second, I refuse to jeopardize my career by dating my boss."

"You say that now, but—"

"Palmer," I said, "you're being ridiculous."

"Maybe."

"You are!" I insisted. "It's you I love."

I wanted to continue defending myself further, but Palmer knew the most effective way to cut me off was to gather me in his arms and kiss me one last time. And, oh, what a kiss it was. He made sure with one single intense meeting of our lips that I would never forget him.

The following morning, I secured the lodge, with the promise to the Brewsters to drop the key in the mail to them upon my return to Seattle. I was down on the dock when the ski-plane landed. Once the engine was cut, the plane coasted on the ice toward me. Sawyer climbed out and tied the plane to the dock because of a mild breeze.

"You must be Josie," he said.

"That's me."

"You ready to go?"

That might well have been the most important question asked of me in my entire life. I couldn't respond verbally, so I nodded. I handed him my gear, and Sawyer

O'Halloran loaded it into the back of the plane, offering me his hand to help me aboard.

Once inside the Cessna, I strapped myself in and looked out the window at Ponder, tears making wet tracks down my cheeks as the engine roared to life. Within a matter of minutes, we were in the air, circling over the lake.

As I looked at the beautiful town in the early sunlight one last time, I saw a lone figure down below. His face was raised to the sky as we flew into the distance.

Even if I hadn't recognized his coat and Hobo at his side, I would have known who it was.

CHAPTER NINE

Palmer

It seemed like forever since Josie flew out of Ponder. In the beginning we talked nearly every day. Long conversations that sometimes lasted up to two hours. I never knew that two people could have so much to talk about, but we did. We shared experiences from our childhoods, and we talked about our hopes for the future, our dreams and goals. Josie kept her promise and didn't mention Chef Anton, and I was grateful.

I had revamped my design for the sword and it was coming along well. I was proud of the work I'd done. Although Josie understood little of my profession, she listened intently as I explained each step of the process and was genuinely interested in what I did. She told me about the menu she'd helped to create, and how well the restaurant opening had gone. There'd been several bumps that needed to be smoothed out with the kitchen and serving staff the first few days. From the sounds of it, she'd handled all the necessary "fixes" professionally without ruffling egos, which is hard to do in that line of work, she said.

As time went on, I could tell she was exhausted, and her calls came later and later in the night. Although I didn't ask, I couldn't help but wonder exactly what the high-and-mighty Chef Anton contributed to the running of the business. From everything Josie said, she bore the brunt of the responsibility and the burden. Admittedly, my knowledge of the restaurant world was completely nil. For all I knew, the chef could be working his fingers to the bone right alongside her.

It was Thanksgiving Day, and Josie had been scheduled to spend the entire day at the restaurant, as it was known to be one of the busiest days in the industry. Missing her the way I did, I had thought about flying into Seattle and surprising her. I decided against it because she was working sixty hours a week or longer and I knew we would have little time together. In fact, we hadn't talked by phone in two days. Quick, short text messages from her still came, but the calls stopped.

Early that morning, I sat at the table in my sister's kitchen, staring at my phone. A brief message popped up from Josie, which shocked me. It was still early in Seattle. Seven in the morning, and she was already at work. The last message I'd gotten from her was just after she left the restaurant at midnight, her time, which meant she had had only a few hours' sleep.

Miss you.

Miss you back.

It's going to be hectic today. I'll call you once I'm home.

I stared at the text, unsure how to respond. She worked so hard, and for what? She'd repeatedly told me she loved what she did. That was all well and good, but these long hours? They had to be killing her.

When's your next day off?

Unsure. Can't talk now. Sorry. Love you.

Exhaling sharply, I flipped my phone upside down on the table, frustrated.

My sister joined me in the kitchen. "You're looking thoughtful for this early in the morning," Alicia said. She had a robe over her pajamas and wore a ridiculous pair of bunny-rabbit slippers.

I'd flown into Fairbanks the day before, looking for an escape from the doldrums that had plagued me since

Josie's departure. Sawyer mentioned that he had to make a trip into Fairbanks to pick up an airplane part and offered to stop for me on the way through. The timing was perfect, and I eagerly joined him, anxious for the distraction.

"It's Thanksgiving, Brother—a day to count our blessings, not our misgivings."

"I know what day it is." But Alicia was right. I should be thinking positive thoughts instead of filling my head with concerns about Josie.

My sister rolled up the sleeves of her robe and opened the refrigerator to retrieve the twenty-pound turkey, setting it inside the kitchen sink. I would have asked if she needed help, but she had it handled.

"You should have let me do that," I mildly chastised her.

"I'm not a weakling, you know."

No one would accuse my sister of that. She was a veteran police officer and was fully capable of taking down a man twice her size.

"How long has it been now?" she asked.

I knew what she was asking but played dumb. "Since when?"

With her hand braced against her hip, my sister turned to face me, her look intense, letting me know she wasn't fooled. "How long has it been since you saw Josie last?"

"Josie who?" I asked, teasing her. Without success, I tried to hold back a smile. The corners of my mouth trembled and were a dead giveaway.

Alicia burst out laughing. "She's got you tied up in knots, doesn't she? Don't try and deny it. She's on your mind night and day, and, little brother, you don't need to tell me you're missing her. I don't know why you're sitting here like a bump on a log when you're clearly wishing you were with Josie."

I could deny it, but it wouldn't do any good. Thankfully, I was saved from answering when Drew, Alicia's husband, entered the kitchen, still dressed in his pajamas. Barefoot, he walked over to the coffee machine.

"Morning," he said, yawning as he opened the cupboard and reached for a large mug. He set it on the counter, wrapped his arms around my sister's middle, and kissed her neck.

"Drew," she protested, "I'm getting the bird ready to put in the oven."

"Yeah, yeah, yeah," he teased, as he continued to nuzzle Alicia's neck.

I noticed how my sister tilted her head to the side and sighed as her husband hugged and loved on her.

I had to look away, but not because their open display of love and affection embarrassed me. Watching them together made me yearn for Josie even more. I would have welcomed the opportunity to love on Josie in the mornings the same way Drew did my sister.

Breaking away from Alicia, Drew poured a cup of coffee and joined me at the table while my sister remained busy prepping the turkey and getting it ready for the oven.

"Before you came into the kitchen, I was asking Palmer about Josie," Alicia said, picking up the conversation that I was trying not to have.

"Josie's in Seattle. She loves her job and she's happy there."

"You sure about that?" Drew asked, taking a drink of his coffee.

"Yes." She'd said as much any number of times, despite the stress of the job. I stopped questioning the long hours or extra responsibilities, because every time I did, she went into a detailed explanation about what was expected of her.

"What have you done lately to let her know you love her?" my sister asked.

"Huh?" Josie knew how I felt. I told her every chance I could.

"You heard me," Alicia insisted. "Sure, you text her and you chat now and again."

Drew leaned back in his chair, taking in the whole conversation while continuing to drink his coffee. "Trouble is, living the way we do in Alaska, men seem to lose a few of the finer social niceties that women are accustomed to. Women want us to give them exotic flowers and French chocolates and say all those sweet words they read in those romance books. They need to hear that we couldn't possibly live without them, and a bunch of stuff like that."

Alicia shook her head. "Would you kindly stop? That isn't what I meant. Josie doesn't need gifts. She needs my brother."

I wasn't sure what my sister was getting at. I wanted to go see Josie in the worst way. I would be in Seattle this very minute if she wasn't involved with the restaurant 24/7.

"Took me three tries to get Alicia to agree to marry me, you know."

I was familiar with their courtship. Alicia and Drew met when she was in college studying criminology. Drew was an electrician doing work on campus in the bookstore where Alicia worked part-time. A few days after they met, he'd asked her out and she'd accepted. At the end of their first date, he proposed. Alicia had been shocked and immediately turned him down. Drew was persistent, though. Two months later he asked her to marry him again, and for the second time, Alicia refused. He waited a year from the day they met and asked a third time. Alicia agreed. They were married three months later, and in the last ten years they'd had two children.

"You aren't giving up on Josie, are you?" Drew inquired.

"No way," I insisted. "She's the one who walked away. She knows I'd marry her in a heartbeat. She needs to be the one to tell me when she's ready. I'm not going to rush her."

"Well, you could help push her along with her decision, don't you realize?" Drew added, not letting up.

"Would you two stop trying to fix this thing between me and Josie?" I snapped, growing irritated. "Josie and I know what we want, and for now, I need to give her time."

"Time? Really, Palmer? And how's that working?" Alicia asked, assuming the role of Dr. Phil. She seemed to want to hammer away at my misery.

Drew shook his head, frustrated with me. "You love this woman or not?"

"I'm not in the habit of asking random women to marry me," I returned sarcastically.

"Look at me, Palmer," Alicia insisted. "I'm your sister. I know you better than anyone. You're in love and you're miserable. Josie's in Seattle, and you're in Ponder. You need to fix this."

Alicia made it sound easy.

"I have to give Josie this chance to work with Chef Anton and run this new restaurant. It's what she wants, it's what she deserves, and I'm not taking that away from her. You want me to show her that I love her? Well, that's how I'm doing it."

My sister went quiet and I noticed Drew had as well. It seemed I'd finally reached them. Was I happy to be separated from Josie? No way. Did I think she was working too long and too hard? Yes. Did I miss our phone chats and extended text messages? More than I was willing to admit. But I couldn't say or do anything until she made her decision. I'd give her a year, and if at the end of that time she was still happy with her life in Seattle, I'd cut my losses and move on. Until then, I clung to the hope that she would have a change of heart and marry me.

"You *do* love her," Alicia said into the silence, as though she found it hard to believe. "You're sincere."

"Of course I am." This was too important to mess up because I was impatient or unwilling to give Josie the time she needed.

"You could always beg," Drew continued, sounding completely serious. "I would have bent down on both knees if it meant Alicia would agree to marry me."

"You did get down on your knees, didn't you?" I inquired.

"One knee," Drew corrected. "If it had taken both knees, I would have gladly done it. Pride is important to a man, but it isn't everything. When it comes to the right woman, a man needs to be willing to swallow his ego every now and then. Not often, mind you, but when the occasion calls for it."

I chuckled, loving both my brother-in-law and sister, and grateful for their support.

Later we lingered around the table after sharing a delicious Thanksgiving dinner complete with turkey, stuffing, and all the fixings. We'd gone around the table and each shared what we were most grateful for in our lives that year, and I'd mentioned my family and friends, including Jack and Josie. Because Alicia had spent most of the day cooking, the rest of us went to the kitchen to wash the pots and pans and load the dishwasher.

"What are you the *most* thankful for, Uncle Palmer?" eight-year-old Andrew asked.

"You helping me with the dishes," I joked, handing him a dishtowel.

"Are you ever going to get married?" little Katie asked. She was six, in first grade, and as cute as a button.

"I hope so," I told her.

"I'd like a girl cousin, okay? Mom and Dad said I can't have a baby sister, so I need you to get me one."

I grinned. "I'll do my best." I could hardly wait to mention this to Josie. On second thought, maybe that wasn't such a good idea.

Drew handed me the last of the pots he'd washed by hand. "The pressure is on," my brother-in-law muttered under his breath. "Not only is Katie looking for a girl cousin, but your parents are looking for more grandchildren. The ball is in your court. Alicia and I have our family."

I swatted the wet towel at his backside. "Josie has to agree to marry me first."

"Will Josie be my aunt?" Andrew asked.

"I don't know yet," I told him, but if I had anything to say about it, then she would be, and soon.

After the dishes were dried and put away, we sat down in the living room, too full to consider pumpkin pie until later that evening. The kids were busy playing a board game, as they were allowed only a certain amount of time on their tablets each day. Sitting on the carpet in front of the fireplace, they involved Alicia in their fun.

Drew and I were caught up in watching the football game when he leaned over and said, "You need a plan, you realize."

I glanced at him and assumed he was talking about Josie and me. "A plan," I repeated. "What sort of plan?"

"To convince Josie to marry you."

"Well, your plan took a while, right?"

"It did, but then, Alicia is stubborn."

"Hey, I heard that!" my sister called from her position on the carpet with the two kids.

I grinned. Being stubborn was a family trait. "Not sure how having a set plan would work with Josie." Pressuring her was the last thing I wanted to do.

The Seahawks scored a touchdown and Drew let out a loud whooping cheer, then added, "All I'm saying is you need to confront this thing with Josie as you would any problem. Have a plan and stick to it."

I smiled. "Is that so?"

"Sure thing. My plan and my persistence paid off with Alicia."

"Drew, I swear if you say another word," my sister interjected, "I'm going to find an excuse to arrest you. Leave my brother be. He's got this under control. Let him figure this out on his own without any help from you."

Drew sighed dramatically. "Yes, dear."

My sister tilted her head back and groaned. "You know I hate it when you say that."

"Yes, my love."

"Better." Alicia got up from the floor and walked over to where Drew reclined in his chair and climbed into his lap. Looping her arms around his neck, she asked, "You know what I'm most grateful for this year?"

He arched his eyebrows. "Your romantic husband?"

"Guess again."

"That it's almost Christmas and you found me the perfect gift?"

"Wrong."

"Okay." Drew sighed. "I give up. Tell me what you're most grateful for this year."

"That my brother has finally fallen in love."

"Aw, Sis," I said, checking my phone, hoping to find a text message from Josie. My heart sank. There wasn't one.

*

I waited until the football game was over and reached for my laptop to go online. Because we communicated daily, I hadn't ever thought to look at Josie's Facebook page, but seeing something new about her life might give me my "Josie fix." I suppose this showed how desperate I was, but I didn't care. I didn't even know if she'd had any time to make posts since beginning work at the restaurant. Alicia happened to walk by, and she paused when she saw that I had logged on to Facebook.

"What are you doing?" she asked.

"Checking Facebook."

"For Josie?"

I nodded.

"Are you sure you want to do that?" she asked.

Now, that was a curious question. "Why do you ask?"

"No reason," she said nonchalantly. I instantly put two and two together and realized that Alicia had been following Josie. The tone in her voice also told me that something was on there that my sister didn't want me to see.

"Do you have something you need to tell me?" I asked my sister.

Alicia exhaled slowly. "You might as well look. You'll find the photo soon enough."

The photo.

134

It didn't take long to uncover the post Alicia was referring to. The instant I caught sight of it, my stomach clenched.

I should have guessed, should have known.

The photo was of Josie and Chef Douglas Anton in front of the newly opened restaurant, Chez Anton. Chef Anton had his arm around Josie. They looked like a couple.

I stared at it for a long time, looking for any indication that Josie might have been uncomfortable with how close he was next to her. As far as I could tell, she appeared to be fine with it.

"Palmer," Alicia murmured. "Say something."

"What's there to say?" I asked. I was the one who'd asked her not to let me know anything about her interaction with the great-and-mighty chef. It all made sense now—why Alicia and Drew insisted that I needed to make my move before I lost Josie. They might be right after all. The phone calls had diminished; the texts were rushed and minimal now.

Then again, maybe I was too late. I might have already lost her and just didn't know it yet.

CHAPTER TEN

Josie

I couldn't wait to get home. I was exhausted and overwhelmed and miserable. It was Thanksgiving Day and I'd spent the last sixteen hours in a hot restaurant kitchen, directing staff, cooking when needed, and inspecting plates before they were handed over to the servers. Chef Anton had departed an hour after we'd opened and left me in charge.

To be frank, Chef Anton had been a huge disappointment. He flitted in and out of the restaurant, although he'd made a commitment to his investors to be a continual presence in the restaurant for the first year at this location. If he did happen to be on-site, he most often was holed up in his office, resenting any intrusion or interruptions, and rarely participating in the day-to-day operations.

I suspected this behavior might be a way to get back at me because I wouldn't return his advances. Almost from the first day I'd returned from Alaska, Chef Anton had hinted that he was looking for something more from me than a normal employee working under him. I made sure he understood I considered this a professional relationship and that I wasn't interested in anything beyond that. It disappointed and discouraged me to realize it wasn't my culinary skills that impressed the chef as much as my bra size. I hated the looks he gave me. Thankfully, his behavior had never progressed beyond those initial remarks. Obviously, I hadn't mentioned any of this to Palmer. He'd made it clear he wasn't interested in hearing anything having to do with Chef Anton, and that turned out to be a blessing in disguise, as my mother would say.

What surprised me was how intuitive Palmer had been about him. And all Palmer had seen was his photograph. One look, and Palmer had read the man like a mystery novel.

I opened the front door to the small home where Mom and I had lived from the time I was born, near the Queen Anne area of Seattle. I was grateful to be home at last and eager to connect with Palmer, despite the late hour. Having to miss Thanksgiving with Mom and my aunt and uncle and their family had been a major disappointment, especially since I'd been in Alaska for close to seven months and had not seen them for so long.

"You're home." Mom sat on the sofa with her feet propped up. "And much later than I expected."

"I know." Flopping down next to my mother, I rested my head against the back cushion and closed my eyes.

"You're exhausted."

I didn't bother answering, figuring it was obvious. I'd left the house early that morning, one of the first to arrive at the restaurant and the last to leave, which was often the case. Since I was the sous-chef, it was expected.

"Did you manage to find time for dinner?"

This was the crazy part. I worked around food all day and rarely got a chance to eat. "Not hungry."

"Josephine Marie, you're skipping far too many meals."

"Yes, Mom." If she could find time in that hectic restaurant kitchen for me to sit down to a meal, then I'd eat. Chef Anton was a hard and unreasonable taskmaster. Already, the station chef had quit without notice, unwilling to take Chef's explosive behavior. The prep cook was the next to go, and two of the waitstaff had quit rather than endure his tirades. The restaurant had been open not even two full weeks and there were already major problems brewing.

"I brought home a plate from your aunt Lucy and uncle Paul's. I had the feeling you were going to go without dinner again."

"Thanks, Mom." I'd eat later. I was far more interested in talking with Palmer. I knew he was spending the holiday with his sister and her family in Fairbanks. I'd texted him before I left the restaurant and was surprised not to hear back from him. In the past he'd always been quick to reply.

"Everyone missed you."

"I missed them, too." I hated not being there with my family for Thanksgiving, even though I knew this was one of the negatives of my career choice.

"What time did you get home?" I asked, hoping to keep Mom talking. Her voice soothed me.

"Around five, I guess."

She hesitated, as if there was more she wanted to say. I'd noticed a change in her since my return. I could be imagining it, though, as I was preoccupied with both work and Palmer.

"By the way, you have a message on the phone," she said, quickly changing the subject. "It's from Jack. I think it might be the friend you mentioned from Ponder."

My eyes shot open and I bolted upright. "Jack called?"

Mom stared back at me, wide-eyed. "I believe that was what he said his name was."

My heart sped like a race-car engine. How I missed Jack. I'd taught him how to use his phone to text me, and he did every now and again, mainly to tell me he was hungry and missed my cooking. Palmer mentioned him occasionally, too. He held a special place in my heart.

"I'd like to know how he got the phone number to the house," Mom commented, as we had an unlisted number.

Mom kept the house phone active because she didn't always have her cellphone close at hand. When I'd applied for the job at the lodge, I'd listed the home phone as my emergency contact number along with Mom's cell number, but I'd written in the house number first. Anyone needing to reach her would have more luck with the house phone. That didn't answer the question of how Jack had obtained access to it, however.

"I'm not sure, Mom."

"He sounded a bit old for you, Josie," my mother teased. She knew I kept in touch with Jack, as well as

Palmer. I hadn't shared the full extent of my feelings for Palmer, unsure myself where the relationship would take us.

"Jack's around your age, Mom."

"That's old."

I waved aside her comment. "He's the hunting guide I mentioned."

"I figured as much. You might want to listen to the message yourself," Mom suggested.

When I'd arrived home, I was convinced I wouldn't be able to move again for a week after sixteen straight hours on my feet. Eager to talk to my friend, I sprang upright and headed to the kitchen, where Mom kept the house phone. The light, indicating a voicemail, was flashing. I reached for a pen in case I needed to write something down and listened to the voicemail.

"Hello? Anyone home?"

I smiled as warmth washed over me at the familiar sound of Jack's froggy voice.

"This is Jack. Jack Corcoran. I hope I have the right number. I'm calling for Josie Avery. It's Thanksgiving Day." He paused, as if expecting someone to pick up and answer. *"Being that it's Thanksgiving and all, I want Josie to know that I'm thankful for her. I wish she was back here cooking for me the way she once did."*

141

I should have known Jack was thinking about his stomach.

"Palmer isn't here. He went to visit his sister and left Hobo with me. Hobo misses you, too, same as me."

Palmer's husky. I longed to wrap my arms around that dog and bury my face in his thick fur. I'd never had a dog as a kid—Mom was fond of cats. I'd grown attached to Palmer's sidekick and missed him, along with everything and everyone in Ponder.

"No need to call back," Jack continued. *"I called to wish you a Happy Thanksgiving and let you know Angie and Steve invited me to dinner with them."*

The call abruptly ended, and I leaned against the kitchen counter. A silly grin covered my face while I replayed the voicemail. Just hearing Jack's voice was like a soothing balm to my tired body. I missed them all. I was willing to admit nothing felt the same since I'd left Ponder. Even being at home with Mom. I'd been away a little more than seven months, and things had changed here: I'd changed. Mom had, too. We'd always been close—still were. But things were different for some reason. I attributed it to missing Palmer, to the long hours at work, and to the pressure of working with Chef Anton.

"Everything okay, Josie?" my mother asked, joining me in the kitchen. She removed the foil-covered dinner plate from the refrigerator and set it on the counter in front of me.

"Everything is peachy," I said, straightening. I should have known better than to try to hide my feelings from my mother. She knew me far too well.

"You miss Alaska, don't you?"

This wasn't the first time Mom had brought up the topic. Rather than answer verbally, I shrugged. The truth was, not a day passed that Palmer and his proposal weren't front and center in my mind. I was surprised by how much of my daily life revolved around thoughts of him. The one bright spot in my days of late were the few text messages we were able to exchange. If I wasn't completely wiped out physically, we used to chat on the phone, until I became consumed with my duties at the restaurant. I had it bad for Palmer.

The only time my head was free of thoughts of him was when I was at the restaurant. I didn't have time to think about anything but getting the food out in a timely manner and serving it up in a fashion befitting Chef Anton's high standard of perfection.

"Josie?" Mom repeated, cutting into my thoughts.

"Yes, Mom, I miss Alaska," I confessed.

"Oh, sweetheart, this job with Chef Anton isn't working out the way you wanted, is it?"

"Not at all." I'd worked in a busy restaurant before I'd graduated from culinary school, so I knew the hours would be long, but working with a man so unreasonable and bombastic was more than I had bargained for.

Mom wrapped her arms around me and gave me a tight hug. "Why don't you return Jack's call? You'll feel better."

I looked at the clock, noting the hour time difference. Then I punched in Jack's number that I found on the caller ID.

The phone rang five times before he answered.

"Jack, it's Josie."

"Josie!" he cried, sounding like I had risen from the dead to contact him. "Oh my goodness, it's so great to hear your voice."

"Yours, too. But I'm curious how you got my home number." I'd never given it to him, although I knew the Brewsters had access to it.

"Ah . . . well, it might be best if you not know in case I get arrested for breaking and entering."

His words alarmed me. "You broke into the lodge?"

"I have a key," he explained. "It's an old one and doesn't fit as well as it once did. I'll be able to fix the door, no problem. Brewsters won't even know there was any damage."

"Jack," I exclaimed, aghast that he would do such a

thing. I recalled that all the office files had locks on them as well. I was certain that Jack didn't have a key to those, but that still didn't explain how he'd managed to get my home number. I didn't really care, though. Hearing his voice was just what I needed.

"Only way I could think to get ahold of you," he explained, sounding more than a little chagrined. "I tried your cell, but that went straight to voicemail."

"It's turned off while I'm at the restaurant."

"You worked today? On Thanksgiving?"

"Yes, it's one of the busiest days of the year in the restaurant business. Is everything all right?" I asked, eager for information. "How's Angie feeling?" My author friend and I kept in touch, too, but I hadn't had time to answer her email from earlier in the week.

"Angie's great. Cooked a good dinner. Lonely around here without you, though, and now with Palmer away, I'm sort of at loose ends. Thought hearing your sweet voice would help."

"I miss you, too," I said, and sincerely meant it.

"Palmer's pretty miserable without you," Jack said. "Don't suppose you'd reconsider marrying him?" he asked, and then expelled his breath. "Don't answer that. Palmer will have my hide for interfering."

Jack had always been an endearing busybody. I could

almost hear Palmer getting after Jack for intruding in his business.

"You happy to be back in Seattle?" Jack asked, changing the subject.

"Oh yes. There's no place like home, right?" That was a slight exaggeration. I'd forgotten how noisy the city could be. The first week home, I'd barely been able to sleep with all the racket at night. If it wasn't the late-night street traffic, it was sirens from emergency vehicles. I didn't realize how much I'd come to appreciate the sounds of silence. I'd grown accustomed to the stillness of Ponder, where one could hear the snow being blown off the tree limbs by the wind, the distant cry of a caribou, and the crackle of the Northern Lights.

"Just curious," Jack said. "You still cooking with that famous chef?"

It amused me the way his mind automatically went to food. "Sure am."

"You ever make moose stroganoff for him?"

"Not yet." I couldn't imagine Chef Anton being interested in tasting my special recipe for moose.

"He'll want to put it on the menu once he tastes it. You tell him I can supply him with the meat if he's interested."

"I'll do that," I said, grinning.

"Well, I best go now," Jack said, appearing to have run out of things to say.

"Nice talking to you, Jack."

"You, too."

I didn't want the conversation to end but I didn't have anything more to tell him.

"Bye now."

"Wait," he said hurriedly. "Did I mention that I miss your cooking?"

"You might have a time or two."

"Oh. Needed to make sure you know that I'm probably losing weight because of it."

That I found hard to believe. "You ever get to Seattle?" I asked him.

He hesitated. "Not in a lot of years. Think I was in the Navy the last time I was there."

"Well, the next time you're in town, you have a standing invitation to come to dinner. I'll cook up a feast you won't soon forget."

"In Seattle?" he asked excitedly.

"Yup. It'd be my pleasure."

"You're on, Josie."

My smile was so big, my mouth hurt as we disconnected the call. I let my hand rest on the phone, my heart warmed by our conversation.

My cell beeped in my pocket. Anticipating it to be a text from Palmer, I quickly reached inside my pocket. It was from my friend Jessie. Not Palmer. Come to think of it, I hadn't heard from him since this morning.

CHAPTER ELEVEN

Palmer

Wouldn't you know it? The minute I stepped off the ski-plane in Ponder and waved Sawyer off, Jack was there to greet me. And who do you think he was talking about nonstop?

Chef Douglas Anton.

Jack had seen a YouTube video with the chef. Who could believe that the old coot even knew what YouTube was, but it was another thing Josie showed him. And who should the chef mention on that video? Josie.

That man was the last person I wanted to hear about, and I'd shut Jack up with a snarl and a cold shoulder. I collected Hobo and speed-walked to my cabin, leaving Jack in the dust. After I cooled down, I felt bad about the way I'd treated him and decided to apologize later.

I'd always known. From the moment I did an Internet search on the chef, I'd sensed he was nothing but trouble. Josie had never hidden the fact that she was thrilled for the chance to work with him. I'd lost count of the number of times she'd told me how lucky she was for this unbelievable opportunity. Not for a minute did I doubt her culinary talents, but in my heart of hearts, I suspected it was more than her cooking abilities that had attracted the chef to Josie.

He wanted Josie. *My* Josie.

My cell dinged with a text message from her.

Everything OK? Haven't heard from you.

I hadn't answered her for a while now. I needed time to think about the Facebook post I'd seen of her with the almighty chef. To hear Josie speak of him, which she'd done plenty of while in Ponder, the man walked on water.

Are you back in Ponder?

It was petty of me to keep ignoring her, so I kept my response short and to the point.

Yes.

Can you talk?

I weighed my options. Earlier I'd been the one to

insist that she tell me nothing about the chef, and if Josie had fallen for him, I wasn't sure I wanted to know it. Mentioning to her that I'd seen the post would be a mistake. The way I currently felt, I'd come off sounding like a jealous fool. *Okay, fine.* I *was* a jealous fool, and unreasonable, too, but I couldn't help how I felt. I had the sinking feeling I was losing her, and I didn't know what to do about it.

I stared at her text again, afraid my attitude would bleed into our conversation.

Sorry. Busy.

Later then?

Sure.

I stuffed my phone back into my pocket, thankful for the delay. My excuse not to chat had validity. The commissioned replica Civil War sword was almost complete. All that was required was putting the finishing touches on the handle.

With my heart heavy, I set to work, welcoming the distraction. Hobo sat on the floor in the workshop, giving me curious looks. Still, my mind refused to let it go. If the photo of Josie and Chef hadn't been bad enough, I'd made the mistake of checking out the chef's Facebook page as well.

That had sent me over the edge. There were photos of

the modern interior of the restaurant and the water view. The kitchen staff were highlighted, including some pictures in which the chef stood next to Josie with a proprietary look about him.

On a positive note, he wasn't holding her against his side like he had every right to lay claim to her, unlike in the photo she'd posted on her Facebook page. My jaw clenched at the memory of her smile in that photo. I wanted to shout at him to remove his arm from around her. Jealous fool that I was, it made me uncomfortable, and that was putting it mildly.

It was a good thing I wasn't talking to Josie just yet. I needed time to process my next move. *A plan,* I decided. I needed a plan. My hand stilled as I admired my work on the sword. I was proud of how it'd turned out and knew the owner would be happy. It was a special Christmas gift that a woman had commissioned for her husband, who was a well-known Civil War historian and Gettysburg battlefield guide. I was confident this beautifully crafted sword would become a family heirloom, passed down from one generation to the next.

Although I'd rarely done it in the past, at Josie's urging, I'd decided to hand-deliver the sword. Flights out of Fairbanks often required a plane change in Seattle.

She and I had discussed me visiting her several times, and Josie seemed eager to see me. Obviously, I felt the same—and then some—about seeing her again, too. This layover in Seattle would be brief. How was I going to prove how serious I was in such a short time span?

I loved her and wanted to build a life with her if she was willing. In my mind I'd given her a year to think about my proposal, but I realized now that a year was too long. She needed to make up her mind, and soon, and I was determined to do my best to persuade her to marry me.

Setting aside the sword, I went into the house and logged on to my computer. I was staring at the screen when Jack let himself in. He didn't say anything at first, and I knew he was probably gauging my mood after the way I'd snapped at him when I'd first arrived back from Fairbanks.

"Sorry about earlier," I mumbled.

"No problem."

"You understood what I was trying to tell you, right?"

He pantomimed zipping his lips shut. "You don't want me to talk about . . . who?"

"Right." I grinned, letting him know I appreciated that I didn't need to explain further.

Jack had never been one to hold a grudge, and he easily accepted my apology.

"What you doin'?" He plopped himself down in the kitchen chair next to me.

"I'm booking a flight," I returned absently, pretending not to notice his behavior.

"To where?"

"Pennsylvania. I'm hand-delivering the sword." My gaze didn't waver from the computer.

"When you leaving? Soon, right? You going to lay-over to see Josie? You probably should; her working with that—" He stopped abruptly, embarrassed. He zipped his mouth with his fingers again.

Feeling the way I did, the last thing I needed was Jack reminding me that Josie spent time with the chef every day while I was over two thousand miles away, twiddling my thumbs and jealous as hell.

"I'm not sure yet when I'll leave. Why?" Jack stretched his neck to get a better view of the screen. He seemed overly curious about my travel plans.

"I got big travel plans myself," he stated casually. "Might work best if we left and returned around the same time. Save costs that way, with Sawyer needing to get us into Fairbanks."

Jack booking a flight? In all the years I'd known him,

he'd never gone farther than a couple hundred miles from Ponder.

"Where are *you* going?" I asked, unable to hide my curiosity.

He rubbed his hand down the side of his beard. "I'd rather not say."

I turned to look at the old coot. "What?"

"My lips are sealed," he reminded me.

If he wanted to keep secrets, that was fine by me. He was welcome to fly wherever he wanted to without my approval. My lack of curiosity was driving him nuts. Jack was practically jumping out of his long johns in his eagerness to tell me. Letting him stew would do him good, so I continued to torment him. "If you want to plan a trip, great; we can coordinate with Sawyer."

He narrowed his eyes until they almost disappeared into his bushy eyebrows. "Thing is, I'd be happy to give you a few details if you really wanted to know."

I shrugged. "Up to you, my friend." I was beginning to think he'd met a woman online and they had planned a rendezvous.

He leaned toward me and lowered his voice to a whisper, acting like someone might be listening in on our conversation. "I'm going to visit Josie."

"Josie?"

"We talked on Thanksgiving."

"She called you?" She'd reached out to me and I'd let the call go to voicemail. She might have assumed something was wrong and reached out to Jack for information. I'd always answered her calls, no matter what.

Looking smug, Jack leaned back in his chair. He crossed his arms and smiled. "Nope. I was the one who phoned her at her home number, since I couldn't reach her on her cellphone."

"You called Josie?"

"Not telling you how I got her house number, in case the authorities are brought in to investigate later."

"What?" I was convinced he said that for shock value.

"Not going to involve you." The self-satisfied look was back on his face. "Don't want you serving time because of something I did."

I raised my hands in a gesture of complete disbelief. I'd known Jack all these years and didn't think there was anything he could do to surprise me. Well, I was wrong. I stared at him, utterly speechless.

"You want to know what she said?" he asked, with a grin that would rival that of the Cheshire cat. I could see that he wasn't willing to give up any more information without me digging for it.

"Okay, fine, tell me what she said."

"I can mention *his* name?"

"No." The word burst out of me in a fit of impatience.

"Okay, then. It was late, and she sounded really tired."

"She's working a lot," I murmured, remembering how exhausted she sounded whenever we spoke. It didn't matter what time of day it was. Mornings or nights. Chef Anton was doing his best to control her life. I realized now that that was all part of his scheme. If she worked sixteen hours a day, she wouldn't have the time or energy to date anyone but him.

"Other than the one who shall remain nameless, she didn't talk about work. She was real happy to hear from me."

I wouldn't have expected anything less. Josie often asked me about Jack; I knew she missed him and that she was on his mind as well.

"Josie invited me to visit her in Seattle; she said she'd cook for me."

That explained why he was looking to book a flight out of Ponder. He was willing to go to the trouble and expense so Josie would cook for him again.

"She said I could visit anytime. I was thinking the sooner the better, you know? Strike while the iron is hot.

And seeing that you're heading that way yourself, I thought I'd tag along."

Not exactly the plan I had in mind. Then again, having Jack accompany me might prove to be an advantage.

"I'm thinking that between us we can convince her to return to Ponder," Jack continued. "She misses us."

"It's something to consider," I agreed, unwilling to commit.

"You're smiling," Jack noted, grinning himself. "First time in a long time."

He hadn't been around when Josie and I were on the phone.

"So you gonna let me fly to Seattle with you?" he asked.

"I'm thinking about it."

"What's there to think about?" Jack argued, his eyes widening. "You want to win back Josie or not? You have to know I'm your best bet."

"That's debatable," I grumbled.

Jack ignored that. His eyes got big. "I've got an idea."

This might prove to be dangerous.

"We'll surprise her," he burst out excitedly. "We won't let her know we're coming and show up at that restaurant where she's cooking. It'll be a little Christmas surprise. What do you think?"

That isn't a bad idea, I thought to myself, and it would give me a chance to see firsthand what her relationship was with the chef.

"Palmer?" he asked, interrupting my thoughts. He stared intently at me, awaiting my response.

I nodded my head in agreement. I hadn't counted on traveling with Jack, but he'd put up a good argument.

His grin was contagious. "As a bonus, maybe we can convince Josie to cook for us. What could be better than that?" he exclaimed. "Think she'll have my stroganoff on the menu?"

"Can't say. Maybe." That was Jack's favorite dish, and Jack claimed no one came close to cooking it as well as Josie.

"I have to go on to Pennsylvania," I reminded Jack. "Seattle is only a layover. I only intend to stay a few days, if that." It all depended on Josie's reaction. If my fears were realized, I didn't plan on sticking around.

"Okay. Go do what you need to do in Pennsylvania and come back to Seattle. I know you're obsessed about that chef guy, so while you're away, I'll do a bit of snooping and give you a report on anything I find out."

Briefly, I considered his proposal, but it didn't sit right with me. I didn't want Jack spying on Josie.

"Thanks, but no thanks. Josie and I will figure this out ourselves."

"You sure?" He didn't look like he believed me.

I assured him I was, but, bottom line: I'd never been less sure of anything in my life.

CHAPTER TWELVE

Josie

"I'm leaving for work now," I called out on my way to the front door.

"Josie." Mom rushed out from the kitchen, rattled and nervous. "I'm gone overnight and won't be back until late Sunday."

"Mom, you've told me this at least three times today." I didn't know what was up with my mother, but it was obvious now that something was going on that she wasn't telling me.

Something was up with Palmer, too. We had barely spoken since Thanksgiving. There'd been a couple brief phone conversations that felt stilted and awkward. I'd asked him both times if there was a problem, and he denied that there was. It was all so strange. We continued to text, but those messages seemed abrupt, almost like hearing from me was an imposition.

"You'll be all right without me?" Mom called after me.

"Of course. Enjoy yourself and don't worry about me."

"Okay." This trip was with Carol, her best friend, to the quaint Bavarian-style village of Leavenworth, tucked away in the Cascade Mountains. Carol and Mom were taking the train and spending the day touring the picturesque shops. Leavenworth was everything Christmas, oozing charm in a festive winter wonderland. Then on Sunday afternoon the train would deliver them back to Seattle. For years, visiting Leavenworth had been a holiday tradition for Mom and me.

Not this year, though. With my work schedule, Mom and I hadn't been able to find time for any of our usual traditions. I hadn't baked a single cookie or made our family's special recipe for handmade chocolates. Mom had baked fruitcake without me, and that just felt wrong. I was missing out on my favorite time of the year.

When I'd entered culinary school, I'd dreamed of creating amazing dishes. While working at the lodge I had free rein in the kitchen and was able to design my own menus. At the restaurant, I was constantly under Chef Anton's thumb, with no creative freedom after the first days of helping him with the original menu. I wasn't allowed any originality, or even a chance to make suggestions to the menu. Because he was so often absent, I'd tried adding my own flair to a dish and had been severely reprimanded. The only reason he'd learned about what I'd done was from a customer who had complimented him. I'd heard from one of the servers that Chef had taken the credit.

I paused long enough to hug my mother. "Have a wonderful time."

"We will." She looked sad and guilty, though.

"Mom, go and enjoy yourself. We'll get to Leavenworth next year." But not if I continued with Chef Anton.

I left the house with frustration growing inside me. This opportunity hadn't turned out to be the career break I'd thought it would be. Then again, to be fair to Chef Anton, my mindset might have been all wrong. While my head and hands were in the work of the restaurant, my heart remained in Ponder with Palmer and all my friends there. I lived to hear from Palmer and feared I was losing him, though I didn't know why. Drowning in doubts, I was agitated and edgy, not getting enough sleep and not taking time to eat.

I couldn't stop thinking about Mom, too. As much as

she loved and supported me, I sensed my mother was ready for me to find a place of my own. She'd grown accustomed to living by herself, making plans with friends, living her own life. All this was good and as it should be. Mom liked having her own space, and by living at home, I seemed to be intruding on her newfound freedom.

It was time for me to move out. I'd changed, too. Living in Alaska, I'd become independent. I loved my mother and was grateful to her, yet I was ready to be on my own also.

When I arrived at the restaurant, Chef Anton was in a rage. The fresh produce truck had arrived and there'd been a mixup with the order. Instead of the broccolini and cauliflower, they'd delivered a triple order of red radishes. Chef was on a rampage, blaming everyone in the kitchen, insisting the mistake had been an attempt to sabotage him and his reputation.

"Out, all of you! Out of my kitchen!" he screeched as I arrived. He looked directly at me and the rest of the crew. "You're all fired. Every last one of you. Leave me." He dramatically waved his hand, dismissing all of us.

The line cooks stood frozen in place, not knowing

what to do. The prep cook stood in wide-eyed terror. Everyone looked to me to resolve the issue.

"Chef, I'm sure we can fix this," I said as calmly as I could manage.

"Fix this. Fifty bunches of radishes. What am I to do with that?" he fumed. "Did you do this?"

"No, Chef. I'm sure it was a mistake on the wholesaler's part." I was the one who'd placed the order, so I reached for the phone and called the local produce company and spoke with the manager. I had him repeat the order back on speaker so Chef would be assured this wasn't an attempt by the staff to undermine him.

Unfortunately, all the produce trucks were currently out making deliveries and wouldn't return until later that afternoon, too late for us to get what we needed for the current menu.

Chef paled at the news. He rammed his hands through his hair. "Radishes. What am I going to do with radishes?"

Immediately a few ideas came to mind, which I suggested. "We could make a radish-and-jícama slaw, melon balls and radish . . . and what about a cucumber-and-radish carpaccio?"

The staff stood stiff and uncertain as I calmly talked down Chef Anton. From previous experience, they knew

I was the only one capable of reasoning with him. He seemed unable to handle even the smallest kitchen crisis. How he'd reached the position of executive chef and to acquire his own string of restaurants was a mystery to me, especially given his temper and his inability to manage emergencies.

Chef Anton glanced at me and then at the rest of the team. "See to it, then," he muttered, before retreating to his office and closing the door.

The entire kitchen staff, from the line cooks to the dishwasher, sighed with relief. When I'd accepted this job, I'd felt it was an honor, which was why I'd agreed to sign a one-year contract. Not even a month into my position, my job had started to feel more like a prison sentence. I wondered if those who hadn't been chosen realized how fortunate they were.

Working together as a team, we managed to open for dinner without a problem, and several radish dishes were specials of the day, thanks to the hard work of the staff. The first two hours went smoothly. I was busy overseeing the orders coming into the kitchen when Lizzy, one of the servers, sought me out.

"Two men at table sixteen are asking to speak to you."

"Two men?" I asked. Normally anyone who requested to meet the chef sought out Chef Anton, not the second in line. No one knew me, other than a few friends and fellow culinary students.

"They said they were personal friends."

"Did they give you their names?" I asked, too busy to leave unless it was necessary.

"No."

"Were they unhappy with their meal?"

"Not at all. One raved about the food."

"And they asked for me personally? By name?" I inquired, as I checked a plate before it was delivered out front.

Lizzy indicated with a nod that they had. "One is older—fiftyish. He's got a beard and his hair is a little long. The other man is younger and clean shaven. And drop-dead gorgeous. I wouldn't mind meeting him in a dark alley." Her eyes brightened with interest.

Could it be Jack? I'd suggested that he come to visit, but I hadn't heard if or when he intended to take me up on my offer. Surely he would have let me know he was flying in beforehand. If it was Jack requesting an audience, then it left me to wonder who the second man could be. Palmer had a beard. He'd once offered to shave it off for me, but I wouldn't ask him to do that, seeing how it offered his face protection in the winter. He kept it neatly trimmed and he looked handsome with it like that.

What if it *was* Palmer?

My hand instinctively went to my heart, hoping to keep it from leaping out of my chest.

"Should I tell them that you're too busy?" Lizzy asked.

"No. No. Tell them I'll be right out."

Lizzy seemed uncertain. "You sure?"

"Yes, very sure." I bit into my lower lip and rushed to the far end of the kitchen, yanking off my stained apron that was over my jacket, as I frantically tried to calm myself. It was sheer luck that I didn't crash into one or another of the staff when I hurried back to Lizzy in panic mode.

Lizzy started to turn away when I grabbed hold of her arm. "How do I look?" I asked, pleading for her to tell me I was as fresh as a daisy and knowing I was anything but.

Her cocked eyebrows confirmed my worst fears.

"Never mind," I cried, shouting instructions to the rest of the kitchen as I ran into the restroom and looked in the mirror. It was worse than I'd thought. Sweat had dampened the hair around my forehead and several curls had escaped my chef's hat. Any makeup I'd applied was long gone by now. With no time to repair the damage, I grabbed my purse and, with shaking hands, reached for my lipgloss and quickly applied it. It would have to do.

Bracing my hands against the bathroom sink, I inhaled a deep, calming breath. No need to be alarmed. It might not be Jack or Palmer. It could be two strangers who simply wanted to meet the chef. But Lizzy mentioned that they had asked for me by name and not Chef Anton.

Taking in a second slow and even breath, I left the restroom and walked through the kitchen as regal as a queen, with everyone bustling about me, trying to get food out in a timely manner. The lights in the dining room were dimmed. The Christmas tree set up in the foyer had large red balls with gold ribbons and white lights. It was ten feet tall. The windows in the dining room looked out over Puget Sound, with twinkling lights beaming from the waterfront below. A ferry was leaving the dock, heading for Bainbridge Island. Except for my disheveled appearance, everything was picturesque and perfect.

As I rounded the corner of the dining room that would lead me to table sixteen, I mentally steeled myself. My eyes automatically went to . . .

. . . Palmer. It *was* him, but a beardless version.

His gaze locked on me in return. It took me a moment to realize that Jack sat across from him.

"Palmer," I whispered, as I approached the table.

Setting his napkin on the table, he stood and held out his hand. I grabbed hold of it, my fingers curling around his as I resisted throwing myself into his arms. I tentatively touched his cheeks, a bit shocked to see him without a beard.

He blushed and seemed a little embarrassed. "Thought you might like to see me without hair on my face."

"You're beautiful."

Jack chuckled. "Going to remember that one. Bet no one ever called you beautiful before, Palmer."

I didn't mean to ignore Jack but was unable to take my eyes off Palmer. He wore a light blue button-down shirt and Dockers. It was the first time I'd seen him in anything other than a plaid wool shirt and work jeans. For what seemed like an embarrassingly long time, we were incapable of doing anything more than staring at each other.

Jack cleared his throat, and I reluctantly broke eye contact with Palmer and turned to greet my friend, who had stood as well. "Jack," I said, hugging him briefly. "You're here!"

"You said I could," he reminded me.

"I'm glad you did, and you brought Palmer." I would be forever indebted to Jack for this.

He winked at me to signal that this was my little surprise, and what a surprise it was.

Because they had already eaten their dinner, out of pure habit I asked, "Did the meal meet with your satisfaction?"

Jack looked to Palmer and stuck out his chest, proud to know me. "She even talks like one of those fancy chefs now."

"She does," Palmer agreed. "Dinner was above and beyond our expectations."

"What is this side dish with a hint of heat?" Jack asked, pointing down to his plate.

"Radish slaw."

"Radish?" he repeated, not quite sure he believed me.

"It's a long story." My eyes returned to Palmer, as I was unable to stop looking at him. Seeing him didn't feel real. From the way his eyes ran over me, I knew he was feeling much the same things I was. Relief. Joy.

He continued to hold my hand, squeezing my fingers, and I squeezed his back. I couldn't remember ever being this happy to see anyone in my entire life.

"Sorry to see there wasn't bear meat on the menu,"

Jack grumbled. "What kind of a restaurant is it that doesn't serve wild game?"

I shared a smile with Palmer. "I'll mention it to Chef Anton and see what I can do."

"You look wonderful," Palmer said, his voice dipping close to a whisper.

I knew his compliment was a slight exaggeration. Working in a hot kitchen, I knew I resembled a piece of overcooked broccoli. Far be it from me to complain; I knew Palmer was really saying that he'd missed me and was happy to see me, no matter what I looked like. It was how I felt about him, too.

"What about me, Josie?" Jack demanded. "Don't I look good? I trimmed my beard. Got on a new shirt, too." He tucked his thumbs under his red braces and extended them away from his chest while he rocked back on his heels. "This is about as dressed up as I get."

"You're a sight for sore eyes," I said, leaning forward and kissing his cheek. "I'm ecstatic to see you both." I wanted to toss my arms around Palmer and kiss him senseless. That, however, was sure to be frowned upon in public while I was still on the clock.

Lizzy sauntered by, and from the look she sent me, I knew she was seeking an introduction.

"Would either of you gentlemen care for dessert?" she asked, eyeing Palmer.

"Dessert?" Jack's face lit up as bright as the lights on the Christmas tree.

"You don't need to ask Jack twice," I said as she handed out the smaller dessert menus. "Lizzy, these are my friends Jack and Palmer from Ponder, Alaska. I worked there before coming to Chez Anton."

"Is it true what they say about men from Alaska?" Lizzy asked, blatantly flirtatious.

"I wouldn't know," Palmer said, practically ignoring her.

I could have kissed him right smack on the lips. Just the way he looked at me told Lizzy he had no interest in her.

Jack read over the dessert menu. "Can I order more than one?"

"You can order as many as you'd like," I told him, so happy to see him I would gladly have delivered every item on the menu if he asked me. "Dessert is my treat." I'd have Chef Anton deduct the cost from my paycheck.

"Can you join us for coffee?" Palmer asked.

Reluctantly I glanced over my shoulder toward the kitchen, although I couldn't see anything from where

I stood. "I . . . I can't," I said regretfully. "I wish I could, but I'm needed in the kitchen."

"What time do you finish?"

"Late," Lizzy answered for me. "Josie is almost always the first to arrive and the last to leave."

Palmer frowned. "What about Chef Anton?" He directed the question to me.

"He isn't as involved as I'd assumed he would be." Another understatement.

"Get out early tonight, then," Palmer prompted.

More than anything, I wished I could. "I'd like nothing better, but the kitchen crew relies on me."

Jack finished giving Lizzy his dessert order and sat back down. He'd asked for three: the maple bread pudding with espresso butter sauce, the dark chocolate/sea salt caramel square, and apple cake with walnut crunch.

"What about you?" Lizzy asked Palmer, with her most alluring voice.

Apparently, she hadn't gotten the hint.

"Nothing, thanks." His eyes held mine. "How late is late?"

"Eleven. Sometimes later," I told him.

"That will have to do," Palmer said.

Jack yawned. "You two will have to meet without me. I'm dog-tired after that flight."

"We could see each other in the morning if you'd rather," I offered Palmer, knowing he must be tired, too. I hoped he would refuse my proposal, even though I felt I had to make it despite how eager I was to spend time with him.

"He can't," Jack answered for Palmer.

"You can't?" I repeated, shocked.

"I leave in the morning," Palmer told me.

CHAPTER THIRTEEN

Josie

"You're *leaving*?" I didn't say anything more, for fear I'd burst into tears. Having Palmer here in Seattle was everything I'd wished for. Everything I'd dreamed of. I learned that Palmer had arrived in town that very day, and if I'd understood Jack correctly, Palmer was turning around and flying out the next day. My heart felt like it was going down in flames.

"Yes, my flight leaves in the morning," Palmer confirmed.

"But ... but so soon?" Having seen him for only this short amount of time was unfair and cruel. I'd sensed something was wrong for the last couple weeks. I'd asked him, and Palmer had repeatedly made excuses for our short conversations and the terse text messages.

I felt anxious to talk things over, but this wasn't the time or the place.

"I'm sorry, Josie. I need to deliver the sword to Gettysburg."

"Of course," I said, doing a poor job of hiding my disappointment.

Lizzy delivered Jack's three desserts and then whispered urgently in my ear, "Chef Anton wants you back in the kitchen."

After weeks of being subjected to the chef's temper tantrums, I suddenly couldn't care less what he wanted, what he demanded. He could take a flying leap into a steaming pile of cow dung as far as I was concerned. My dreams of a big career move, of working with this renowned chef, weren't working for me. This job was nothing like what I'd been led to believe. I stood, unable to move, struggling not to grab on to Palmer and not to beg him to stay in Seattle.

"Chef isn't happy," Lizzy whispered as she stepped away from the table.

"Tough," I whispered back. If this was all the time I would have with Palmer, I wasn't wasting a single second. My heart ached with everything I wanted to tell him, with all the things I wanted to say, and now I was being cheated of that.

"He's coming back, you know," Jack announced, digging into the bread pudding first and then taking a bite out of the apple cake before shifting to the third dessert.

I looked at Palmer. "You are?"

"I'll be back in three days."

"Three days?" I repeated.

"It takes all day to fly across the country, then one day in Pennsylvania, and another to fly back to the West Coast."

Relieved to hear that he wasn't taking any more time than necessary and was coming back to me, I asked, "You finished the sword?" He'd mentioned his work on it, but lately he'd been using that as an excuse to cut our conversations short.

He nodded and looked pleased with himself. "It turned out even better than I hoped."

"I knew it would." I remembered how frustrated he'd been when he'd discovered the crack before I'd left Ponder. "Then you'll be back?" That would only leave a few days before Christmas. "Can you stay for Christmas?" I blurted out. "You could meet my mother and I'll cook a wonderful dinner for all of us and—"

"You want me to spend Christmas with you?"

"More than anything," I nearly shouted, and I immediately lowered my voice, not wanting to appear overly eager. "Please say you'll stay."

He hesitated, and for one heart-wrenching moment, I thought he would refuse. I was afraid I wouldn't be able to hide my reaction if he did.

Palmer's look grew thoughtful, as though he wasn't sure. "I didn't intend to stay more than a couple days. I've already got plane reservations to return to Alaska."

"I'm sure they can be changed."

"*I* can stay for Christmas," Jack volunteered readily. "What are you planning to cook? The traditional prime rib dinner is fine with me, although I have a hankering for turkey and stuffing, if that's in the offering."

I barely heard him.

"And I'm not that fond of ham," Jack continued, "but if that's what you decide you want to serve, I won't complain. You might already have guessed this, but I'm not picky when it comes to food." Jack looked at me and then at Palmer. "You did invite me to stay, didn't you, Josie?"

"Of course, Jack."

"Good," he said, obviously relieved that the invitation included him. "For a minute there I thought you only wanted Palmer."

"You're welcome anytime, Jack," I assured him.

"Wonderful! What time should I arrive for breakfast?"

Behind me I heard a commotion taking place in the kitchen. I wanted to groan, knowing Chef Anton was on another one of his rampages. His loud voice spilled into the dining area, causing the room to go silent.

Palmer's eyes connected with mine and he frowned. I wanted to explain but didn't dare take the time. "I'll meet you outside the restaurant at eleven," I said, reluctantly leaving my friends to rush back to the kitchen before any more damage transpired.

Palmer seemed to have a hard time releasing my hand, and I was just as hesitant to leave him. He seemed like he was about to say something, and then apparently changed his mind.

Sure enough, the kitchen was in chaos. Chef Anton was shouting at one of the line cooks, waving his arms and making no sense whatsoever. When he saw that I had returned, he whirled on me.

"You are forbidden to go into the dining room."

"I was greeting friends from out of town," I explained, hoping that would placate him.

"I don't care if it was the Pope."

I couldn't believe my ears. It wasn't my habit to desert my post. One time. For friends. I'd listened to his verbal abuse for weeks and I was finished. Done. I'd had enough. More than enough.

"When was the last time you were in the kitchen or at the restaurant for more than an hour or two?" I asked him, my hands digging into my hips. "This is *your* restaurant bearing *your* name. Investors have entrusted you and you're nowhere to be found. When I interviewed for this job, it was understood you would oversee the kitchen for the first year. When you do bother to show up, you're either high or drunk."

I noticed the kitchen crew nodded in agreement, although no one else said anything.

"You agreed—"

"I agreed to this position with the understanding that you would be my mentor. I had no idea that I'd be running an entire restaurant on my own and—" I wasn't allowed to finish.

"You signed a contract, so if you think you're going to walk out on me now, then I will sue you into the next century."

He made the threat sound all too real, and I had to admit it caused me to think twice. In only a matter of seconds, however, I realized he had no grounds to take me to court. "The contract says nothing about being subjected to your abuse or taking on a dozen duties that would normally go to the executive chef. This," I said, making a sweeping gesture around me, "isn't my full responsibility. It's *yours*. It has your name on it, and your recipes. I was hired as a sous-chef, not the executive chef."

Chef Anton glared at me, his eyes spitting fire. "I am giving you an opportunity of a lifetime—"

"*Responsibility* of a lifetime, you mean, but with none of the benefits. I'm finished." I stripped off my apron and tossed it into the garbage can.

The chef tried to block my exit. "I will sue you for every penny you ever hope to earn."

"Then sue me. You've already fired me any number of times anyway, breaching the contract yourself." He wouldn't have the nerve to press a lawsuit, and I knew it. Especially since he'd fired me that very morning when the wrong vegetables were delivered. I had witnesses who would gladly testify against him. Chef Anton had made no friends with the kitchen staff because of his volatile nature. The man was unstable.

I turned to walk out of the kitchen when three of the crew, who had simultaneously removed their aprons, joined me.

"If Josie quits, then I do, too," the line chef declared.

"And me."

"Same here."

Chef's face turned the color of ripe beets. "I'm suing you all. You'll regret this, every last one of you," he raged. "Get back here. You can't leave until I say you can."

Once I was outside the kitchen, I experienced the most freeing of sensations. I felt lighter than air. My one regret was that I had quit in the middle of a shift, but it was what Chef Anton deserved. Although I hadn't shared my suspicions with my mother or any of the other staff, I believed Chef Anton had some sort of drug addiction, and that slowly, over time, he'd become incapable of dealing with the intense pace of the restaurant industry. It was sad to see such a great talent go to waste.

I hurried to collect my belongings and rushed out, hoping to catch Palmer and Jack. My heart fell when I saw that they had already left the restaurant.

I returned to the restaurant at eleven to meet Palmer and by unspoken agreement we walked along the Seattle waterfront, which was beautifully lit up for the holiday season. Happy to be with Palmer, I chatted nonstop; it seemed like forever since we'd talked.

When I realized I was the only one speaking, I felt I had to ask: "You aren't saying anything?"

He grinned. I didn't know if I'd ever get used to seeing him without the beard. I had to resist touching his face.

"It's hard to get a word in," he said, teasing me.

Laughing, I leaned against his shoulder, so content it was hard to hold all that joy inside me. "I have been talking a lot, haven't I?" I knew I should tell him about my run-in with the chef and that I'd abruptly quit my job. The relief was overwhelming. I felt free for the first time in weeks. The weight off my shoulders made me feel like I could take off and fly.

In time I would tell Palmer everything; he deserved to know. But not now. Not when we hadn't seen each other in so long. I wanted to enjoy these few hours we had before he left for the East Coast. The last thing I wanted was to weigh down our conversation with heavy subjects. There would be time for that later. For now, I simply wanted to bask in his company.

We strolled past the ferry dock, my arm wrapped around his elbow. I could see a ferry halfway across Puget Sound, heading to Bainbridge Island. The sight was one I would never tire of seeing.

I'd purposely stopped talking, giving Palmer an opportunity to contribute to the conversation. After a few minutes he told me he'd changed his flight back to

Alaska so there would be plenty of time later to discuss our future. Then he grew quiet again, although he kept me close to his side. I had to wonder at his mood, and then realized there was probably a good reason he seemed withdrawn and reticent.

"You're tired, aren't you?" It made sense, seeing that he had only just arrived in town. It'd been a long travel day for him and Jack. He must be exhausted.

"A little."

"Do . . . would you rather go back to the hotel? We can meet up again once you return from Pennsylvania." I made the offer and sincerely hoped he'd decline. I wasn't ready to let him go.

"No. I want to be with you."

I immediately felt better. "And I want to be with you, too." Lights from the Kitsap Peninsula glowed in the distance. The waterfront Ferris wheel was still lit up, I noticed as we strolled past.

My stomach growled, reminding me that I hadn't eaten since that morning.

Palmer must have heard it, because he asked, "Did you have dinner?"

"No."

"Then let's find you something to eat."

We decided to go to an all-night diner close to Queen

Anne Hill that I knew about. We sat next to each other, holding hands. Palmer seemed more at ease now, and we talked until shortly before one. I yawned and then he did, too, and although reluctant, it was time to call it a night.

We parted, neither of us wanting to leave. I could tell Palmer wasn't quite himself; he admitted he hadn't been sleeping well but didn't mention the reason. Perhaps he had held back from telling me something, too.

Palmer walked me to my car, and under the light post drew me into his arms and kissed me. My eyes filled with tears. I hadn't realized how much I missed being in his arms or how empty my life had felt without him. I clung to him and we held each other for several moments until the taxi appeared that would return him to his hotel.

CHAPTER FOURTEEN

Palmer

Seeing Josie again was everything I'd hoped it would be. My doubts, which had plagued me ever since Thanksgiving, were somewhat quieted. I felt reassured, although not completely. Her immediate reaction when she saw me couldn't be faked. When she'd walked into the dining room from the kitchen dressed in her white double-breasted chef's jacket, it had taken every ounce of restraint I possessed not to pull her into my arms. I desperately needed to kiss her, with a longing so deep my body ached.

Our eyes had locked on each other like magnets. An atomic bomb could have gone off and I wouldn't have been able to look away. I had it bad, worse than I'd been willing to admit. I'd felt a void after she'd left Ponder, and even with our conversations and texting, it wasn't the same.

Josie wanted me to remain in Seattle over Christmas. She hadn't needed to ask me twice. I hadn't allowed her to see how pleased I was at her invitation. As soon as I was back at the hotel before I met her following her shift, I'd called the airlines and changed my return flight to Alaska. I'd been foolish to think one abbreviated evening in Seattle would be enough time to see her. I'd let my ego get in the way of common sense.

The entire time I was in Pennsylvania she was on my mind. I found it interesting that in the short hours we'd spent together she hadn't mentioned Chef Anton once. I hadn't brought him into the conversation, either, preferring to concentrate on Josie and being with her. What worried me was how proud she was of Seattle and how happily she'd pointed out the sights as we walked along the waterfront.

Once I arrived on the East Coast, I conducted my business as quickly as possible and headed back to Seattle with an eagerness I couldn't hide.

The long flight back seemed interminable. The Boeing 737 bounced against the runway as I finally landed in Seattle. I was anxious to see her again, but it would need to wait until after she finished her shift at the restaurant. I'd been patient this long—another few hours shouldn't matter.

Once I was off the plane, I grabbed a taxi and headed back to the hotel that Jack and I had booked in the heart of downtown Seattle. I hadn't talked to my friend while I'd been in Pennsylvania. Jack rarely had his phone handy, which drove me nuts. I was dying to hear what he'd learned from Josie.

As soon as I checked in to the hotel and got my room, I dialed Jack. He answered on the first ring, almost as if he was sitting on the bed, awaiting my call.

"It's Palmer."

"How'd it go?" Jack asked.

"Fine. Have you seen Josie?"

"Sure. Been with her every day since you left for Pennsylvania. She took me to that big farmers' market they got here. It was something. Never seen so much fruit, vegetables, and flowers all in one place. They do tricks with fish, tossing salmon back and forth like it's a seafood ping pong game." He barely paused to take a breath. "Then she took me on the monorail. That was fun, riding up above the streets. She wanted me to go up the Space Needle, but we ran out of time."

That Josie had time to play tour guide surprised me.

I had the impression she worked a lot of hours. I vaguely remembered the server mentioning Josie was the first to arrive at the restaurant and the last to leave.

"Guess what else?" Jack asked, breaking into my thoughts.

"Jack, please, don't play these games with me. If you have information, just give it to me, will you?" I was impatient, and more than a little jealous that it was Jack, not me, who had been able to spend what sounded like an unlimited amount of time with Josie.

"Josie quit her job. Walked out in the middle of the shift the very night we were there." Jack chuckled, obviously finding the entire situation amusing. "She told Chef Anton she could no longer work for him. Between you, me, and the totem pole, I think he was putting all kinds of pressure on her, and some of it didn't have to do with her work in the kitchen."

Funny she hadn't mentioned that to me later that same night, which left me to wonder if there was a reason she'd omitted the news. I guessed it was because she feared what I'd do if I found out that he'd harassed her. For Josie to quit in the middle of a shift spoke volumes. A dozen scenarios flashed through my mind, none of them good. I hadn't liked the look of Anton the minute I'd read his bio. I'd had a bad feeling from the start but feared my judgment had been clouded by my jealousy.

"Do you know what happened?" I asked between clenched teeth. "Did that chef try anything with her? Because if he did . . . I swear, Jack, I don't know that I can let that go."

"Don't go ballistic on me. All Josie would say about the chef was that he was a major jerk. I asked, but she didn't give me details. I could tell that she didn't want to talk about it."

I needed to find out why, and if Josie wouldn't tell me, then I'd pay the chef a visit myself and the two of us would talk, man to man.

All at once I realized what it might mean for us if Josie was no longer working at the restaurant. Hope swelled inside my chest like a water-soaked sponge. Perhaps she'd changed her mind and was reconsidering my proposal. It became impossible to remain sitting, and I sprang to my feet. I needed to see her, talk to her, convince her that we could make our lives together work.

"Her mom invited us to dinner tomorrow night," Jack continued, unaware of my excitement. "I'm looking forward to meeting her. She's been at work and I haven't had a chance yet. You're coming, aren't you?"

"Sure, I'd like that." I was impatient to get a read on Josie, to make sure she was okay, and to find out what quitting her job would mean for her, for us.

Whatever had happened, I needed to play by the book, remembering my talk with Drew and his advice. He'd suggested that I not propose again until I could be sure Josie would accept. The signs were good, but I didn't want to get ahead of myself.

"You ready to eat?" Jack asked.

I looked at the time. It was no surprise that Jack was thinking about his stomach. "It's not even five o'clock yet." Because I was on East Coast time, I was willing to consider an early dinner—early for the West Coast, that is.

"I found this great fish-and-chips place on the waterfront. Lots of tourists there, but the food is worth the wait."

"You know how I feel about crowds," I reminded him.

"Not fond of them myself."

"Do you know what Josie's doing tonight?" I wanted to see her. She knew I was due back today, but not when I was supposed to land in Seattle. I'd held this vision in my mind of her waiting at the hotel for me.

"She's got a previous engagement."

"What?" I burst out. "She's going out on a date?"

192

"Not a date—evening plans with some gal pals. That's what she called them. Some silly-sounding Christmas sock exchange she does every year. She didn't think she'd be able to do it, but now that she isn't working, she's able to go. You didn't answer my question," Jack reminded me. "You ready for dinner or not? It's been hours since I last ate. I was hoping the line for the fish-and-chips place wouldn't be long this time of the day."

I lost my appetite with the news I wouldn't get to see Josie. Sitting alone in the hotel room didn't appeal to me, either.

"I'll meet you in the lobby," I said, riding a roller coaster of emotions.

Hanging up the phone, I made sure I had my key card and headed down the long hallway toward the elevator.

Once in the lobby I paced restlessly, waiting for Jack.

Then, from the other side of the lobby, I heard someone call my name.

I turned toward the voice and saw Josie. Right away she sprinted across the open space toward me and all but launched herself into my arms. I was caught off guard, and she nearly knocked me off my feet. Anyone watching might suspect it'd been months since I'd last seen her instead of only a few days. I held her against me, closed my eyes, and breathed in the scent of vanilla and strawberries in her hair.

"That was the longest day and a half of my life," she whispered, almost as if she hadn't wanted me to hear her admit it.

I would have kissed her if half the lobby hadn't taken an interest in our reunion. "You missed me?" I asked.

"Every single second," she confessed with a soft sigh.

The disappointment I'd felt earlier left me. She'd been thinking about me while I was away with the same anticipation I'd felt on the other side of the country.

"What are you doing here? I thought you had plans this evening."

"I do. With my three best friends. I haven't seen them in months and I wasn't sure what time you'd be back. Jack couldn't remember, and I've been in desperate need of girl time."

I did my best to hide my frustration. It was selfish of me to want her all to myself. She hadn't seen her friends in months, and I couldn't begrudge her this evening, despite my own need to be with her.

"What brought you here to the hotel?"

"I was going to leave a card for you at the front desk, but then I saw you and, well, I had to let you know." Her eyes were wide and inquiring.

"Let me know what?" I asked. She'd lost me somewhere between the hug and the reason for her being here.

"How crazy I am about you and how miserable and lonely I've been without you." Her eyes were warm and sincere. "We had such little time to talk when you first arrived, and you were so quiet. It wasn't until later that I realized that you'd been that way ever since Thanksgiving. It felt like everything changed. When I called, you were too busy to talk for more than a few minutes. Your text messages were short and to the point, too, nothing like they had been earlier. When I asked, you said it was because of the commission. Then you were here in Seattle and you seemed distant and distracted. It's something more, isn't it?"

I could try to hide my insecurities, but at the same time I knew Josie deserved the truth. I held her gaze and told her what was on my mind. "I saw the photo you posted on Facebook with you and Chef Anton," I admitted, holding her loosely and breathing into her hair. Showing weakness went against every instinct I had, but Josie deserved the truth. "I was jealous and afraid I was losing you the way I always feared I would."

"Oh Palmer, if only you knew."

I believed I had a good idea of what had happened.

"Jack says you quit your job. What did that man do to you, Josie?"

She shook her head. "Nothing. Everything. It's a story for another time."

"Josie!" Jack shouted with surprise, joining us. "Didn't think we'd see you tonight."

"I'm only here for a few minutes. I stopped by to leave a card for Palmer to welcome him back and found him in the lobby."

"What's the card for?" Jack asked.

"Oh, I forgot to give it to him. It's an invite to dinner tomorrow night."

"What is your mom cooking?"

Leave it to Jack to be worried about his next meal.

"It's one of her specialties. Don't worry, you'll like it."

Personally, I couldn't imagine Jack taking a dislike to anything homemade.

Josie's eyes reconnected with mine. She smiled, and I swear I could have dropped to one knee and proposed on the spot. She radiated happiness; seeing her was everything.

"Mom is looking forward to meeting you both," Josie said, having trouble keeping her eyes off me.

"Thank her for the invite," I said.

"I will." She looked at the time and her shoulders

deflated. "I need to go or I'll be late for the party. My friends have been after me to get together ever since I got back from Alaska. I can't disappoint them, although . . ."

I could see her struggling, torn between spending time with her gal pals and wanting to be with me.

"Go," I urged. "I'm not going anywhere."

"Yes, go and have a great time," Jack insisted. "You deserve a bit of fun, and it is the holiday season. You don't need to worry about the restaurant or Chef Anton ever again."

I noticed the way Josie stiffened at the mention of the chef's name, which made me more determined than ever to find out what the other man had done to upset my girl.

Even though Josie was in a rush, I had to know. Placing my hands on both her shoulders, I asked, "Tell me, Josie, what's the real reason you quit?"

She shook her head and avoided eye contact. "It's water under the bridge. I don't want to talk about it, okay?"

I wanted to shout, *"No, it isn't okay!"* but I could tell this was a subject she preferred to avoid. I would have to let it go. For now. "Just answer me one thing: Did the chef try anything with you personally?"

"If you mean anything that made me . . . uncomfortable, then not really. You were right to suspect he wanted to . . . date me."

Date. That was a delicate way of saying what I knew she meant.

I'd known it all along. I certainly wasn't surprised to learn he'd been pressuring Josie. She was beautiful, funny, and smart . . . I could go on and on. Working side by side with Josie, Chef Anton would have found it impossible not to be attracted to her. I couldn't fault him for that. Although, if the chef had tried anything unwanted, then he and I would need to have a discussion.

"Did he pressure you?"

"A little."

"Why do I think you're downplaying what happened?" I asked her.

"Palmer, please, drop it. That was only a small part of the overall problem. As soon as he fully understood I wasn't interested, he left me alone."

Relieved, I walked Josie outside to the front of the hotel. "Can I see you tomorrow?" I asked.

She bit into her lip, looking torn. "I've got two job interviews scheduled. I'm sorry, Palmer. I'd really like to spend time with you, but I need another job, and the sooner the better. I'll see you tomorrow night. All the rest of my time is free through Christmas, I promise."

My heart sank. If Josie was on a job search, then that told me she wouldn't be returning with me to Ponder. I swallowed down my disappointment, discouraged but unwilling to show it.

"It's fine, Josie, don't worry."

She impulsively hugged me before scurrying off down a busy Seattle sidewalk, getting lost in the crowd.

Jack joined me. "She's something special, isn't she?"

"Yeah," I agreed. A businessman rushing past bumped into me and caused me to stumble. "Let's get out of here," I said. "All these people are making me feel claustrophobic." If this was what it was like every day in the city, I didn't know how I would last until Christmas. Ponder had never called out my name louder than it was right at that moment, in spite of having the woman of my dreams here in the big city.

"Don't know where all these folks come from," Jack complained.

"Me neither," I agreed, uncomfortable and longing for home. I'd already had enough of people and airports and Christmas in the city.

"I bet the majority have never even tasted the finer things in life, like caribou meat."

"Probably not," I agreed, grinning.

"They do have good fish-and-chips here, though. I'm ready to eat. What's the holdup?"

I grinned, put my arm around his shoulders, and walked with him down to the Seattle waterfront.

The following evening, we took a cab to the address Josie had given Jack for dinner with her mother. The house was in a quiet neighborhood with an amazing view of the city lights. Lots of the families had Christmas lights on their homes, along the rooflines, on porch decks, and around tree trunks. Decorated Christmas trees were visible in the large living room windows. A couple of the yards had big blow-up holiday figures on their front lawns. All this outdoor decorating didn't make a lot of sense to me. In Ponder we had nature giving us displays all through the holiday season, with a multitude of stars randomly tossed like bright dust across the night sky, punctuated by the aurora borealis.

Jack rang the doorbell while I held on to the bouquet of flowers Jack and I had purchased at Pike Place Market earlier that afternoon. The day had been long and mindless. I'd filled the time walking along the waterfront. Jack and I had gone into the IMAX theater and toured the market. All the while I'd wondered if Josie had gotten either of the jobs she'd interviewed for, and what that would mean for us if she did.

Josie answered the door and greeted us with a huge grin. "You're right on time."

She should know by now that Jack had never been late for a meal in his entire life.

As we entered the cozy, warm living room, a middle-aged woman stepped out of the kitchen. She wore an apron decorated with holly berries tied around her waist, over dark pants and a red sweater. I was struck by the family resemblance and knew without an introduction that this was Josie's mother.

"Mom," Josie said to her mother, while moving to stand next to me. She wrapped her arm around mine. "This is Palmer and Jack, my friends from Ponder. Palmer and Jack, this is my mom, Gina Avery."

"I'm pleased to meet you," I said to Gina, and handed her the flowers we had bought at Pike Place.

"How thoughtful," she said, accepting the bouquet. "Thank you, Palmer."

"Thank you for the dinner invite," I said.

Jack hadn't said a word. I looked over and saw that he stood completely immobile. His eyes were wide and focused solely on Josie's mother.

"Jack," I said under my breath. "This is Josie's mother."

He continued to stare until I elbowed him in the ribs.

Jack stumbled forward as though in a trance. "Hello," he said, in a voice I didn't recognize.

Josie looked at me, curious about what had happened to Jack. I couldn't explain it myself.

"Someone should have warned me," Jack whispered.

I wasn't sure he was talking to me. *Warned him of what?*

CHAPTER FIFTEEN

Josie

Something had happened to Jack. He couldn't stop staring at my mother. He hardly touched his meal, and that certainly wasn't like him. The man was all about food. Palmer sat next to me at the table. We exchanged more than one troubled look, because Jack obviously wasn't himself.

"Dinner was delicious," Palmer mentioned when we'd finished the Guinness potpie. It was one of Mom's specialties and a family favorite.

"You outdid yourself, Mom." I added my own compliments, as she knew how important this evening was to me and had pulled out all the stops. I'd prepared baked Alaska for dessert, knowing Palmer would enjoy my choice.

"I'm glad you enjoyed the meal," Mom told Palmer,

and looked across the table at Jack. "You ate very little, Jack. Would you like me to fix you something else?"

Transfixed, Jack shook his head.

"You're sure?"

Jack hadn't said more than a few words since he walked in the door. I had no idea what had come over him.

Mom started to get up from the table and Jack fairly flew out of his seat and raced over to where she sat to pull out her chair.

My mother graciously smiled up at him. "Thank you, Jack." She sent an inquisitive glance at me and I shrugged, not knowing what to tell her.

What happened next shocked me even more. Standing behind her, he leaned over and sniffed her neck.

"Jack!" Palmer cried. "What in the love of heaven are you doing?"

Mom frowned, not knowing what to think of Jack's behavior.

"You're smelling me," Mom said, twisting around to look at Jack.

Jack's eyes pleaded for forgiveness. "I'm sorry. I'm sorry. I wanted to know if you had a human scent. I can't believe you're real."

"Real? Jack, buddy, what's come over you?" Palmer asked gently.

Jack's face, or what I could see of it outside of his beard, had turned a deepening shade of red. "Your mother looks like an angel."

Mom blushed. "I can assure you I'm not." She reached for her plate to carry it into the kitchen, but Jack wouldn't allow it. He grabbed it out of her hand and then took his own plate and followed behind Mom like a lost puppy.

"What's with Jack?" I asked Palmer. It was just the two of us at the table now, and he looked as perplexed as I did.

"This is crazy," Palmer agreed. "I've never seen him like this."

"Are you sure? You've known him for years. It's like he's walking around in a fog."

A couple minutes later, Jack returned to the dining room. He paused in the doorway, looked at Palmer and me, pressed his hand over his heart, and nearly swooned.

"I'm in love," he declared.

"Jack, you just *met* my mom," I replied, determined to talk sense into him. One look at the way his eyes had glazed over told me he wasn't ready to listen. Whatever it was about my mother that had entranced him remained a mystery. I could tell she was flustered at Jack's attention.

Jack sat down across from us, crossed his arms on the table, and leaned forward to whisper, "The minute I set eyes on your mother, I felt this thing happen in my gut, like the flu bug hit me worse than any sickness I've ever had, worse than the bubonic plague."

His love analogy could use a little work. No woman wanted to be compared to a pandemic.

"Did you see what happened to me? It was like I got hit with a sledgehammer."

Again, his expression of love needed a tad bit more finesse.

"Your reaction to Gina was hard to miss," Palmer told him, understating the obvious.

"I know. My tongue wouldn't work and all I could do was stare. I couldn't even touch my food! Even now I can't believe that Gina isn't a heavenly being, and that she's actually a human."

"What on earth prompted you to sniff her neck?"

Jack had the good grace to look embarrassed. "She forgave me like the angel she is."

"Take my advice and don't try it a second time," I warned him. I knew my mom wouldn't put up with that for long.

Leaning forward, Jack lowered his voice, as if his next words were of great importance. "Josie, I've got to know, and please be honest."

Palmer and I shared a concerned look. *Know what?*

"Do I have a chance with your mother?" If he leaned any farther over the table, he'd have his face in the salad bowl. He eyes implored me to give him hope.

Not knowing what to tell him, I silently sought Palmer's help. He knew Jack far better than I did. "I . . ."

Palmer held up his hand, stopping me. "Can you give Josie and me a minute to discuss this?" he asked his friend.

Jack glanced from Palmer to me and then back again before he agreed.

"In private," Palmer clarified.

"In private," Jack echoed. He pushed back the chair, moved into the living room, and paced in front of the Christmas tree. He reminded me of an expectant father awaiting the birth of his first child.

"What should I tell him?" I asked Palmer, not wanting to hurt or discourage Jack. At the same time, I wanted him to realize his behavior had likely worked against him as far as my mother was concerned. Jack was great, but as much as I cared about him, I couldn't imagine my mother with someone like Jack. Mom was a city girl, even more than I was.

"Maybe you should talk to your mother, ask her," Palmer advised.

"Good idea." The only logical one. Besides, I should

be helping my mother with making coffee. She'd gone into the kitchen and I'd intended to follow her. I would have if Jack hadn't practically tripped over a chair in his eagerness to be of help.

"You go in with your mother," Palmer suggested, "and I'll do what I can to reason this out with Jack."

We each left the table.

I found Mom leaning her hip against the countertop, tapping her index finger against her lips while deep in thought. She didn't seem to notice that I'd entered the kitchen. Again, I wondered if there was something or perhaps someone that Mom wasn't telling me about. My suspicions were raised when I'd asked her about her trip to Leavenworth. Her responses had been vague, and she'd quickly changed the subject, which was unlike her. She always loved telling me about her adventures after coming home from a trip. It all felt odd to me. I'd wanted to get to the bottom of what was happening, but there hadn't been a chance.

"It appears you have an admirer in Jack," I said. Mom stood next to the coffeepot, which had just finished brewing. Two cups and saucers, plus two mugs, sat in front of it.

"He seems sincere," she said, smiling. "I don't mind telling you that your friend is a little odd."

"Jack's sincere—I promise you that, all right—although Palmer and I are hard-pressed to explain his behavior." I wasn't sure how to read her. We'd always been open and honest with each other . . . or had been. "Jack asked if he had a chance with you; I don't know what to tell him."

"He lives in Alaska," Mom declared. "And not just Alaska, but in Ponder. How far did you say this town was from any hint of civilization?"

"A few hours. It's a nice little town, and after a while you hardly notice the lack of amenities." The more time I spent away from Ponder, the more I missed the easy life there. The more I missed Palmer.

"Josie, honestly, I just met this man, and even if . . . He's a dear, don't misunderstand me. I'm flattered by his attention, but really, can you honestly see me living anywhere but here? Jack and I obviously live in two very different worlds."

I agreed with her. "Don't worry, Palmer is talking to him now, hoping to let Jack down easy."

"He's very sweet."

Sweet wasn't exactly the word I'd use. I certainly wasn't going to tell my mother that Jack felt like he'd been hit with a virus the minute he set eyes on her.

"Let me help you with the coffee," I said, reaching for

the glass pot. Knowing how both Jack and Palmer liked theirs served, I doctored each one. I was about to suggest we serve dessert, although I didn't think anyone was close to being ready. Depending on Jack, it might be a good idea to make an early night of it.

Admittedly, I was disappointed at how this dinner had gone. Palmer and I hadn't had a moment to ourselves yet.

Mom and I carried the coffee into the living room, where Jack and Palmer sat waiting. Jack was on the sofa, leaning forward, his head in his hands. Hearing us, he looked up, and when he saw Mom, he released a low moan like he was in pain.

"Gina," he whispered.

You'd think a ghost had just drifted into the room, not my mom.

"Here's some coffee," Mom said, setting his mug down on a coaster on the coffee table. "Would anyone like to listen to Christmas music?"

Jack nodded. Once again, words appeared to have escaped him.

Mom reached for the remote and then turned on the music to a low but discernible volume.

Palmer stood next to the fireplace where our stockings were hung. My grandma Warren had knit mine when I was ten. Mom had hers from when she was little, too.

Palmer took the mug out of my hand and I sat in the chair closest to the Christmas tree.

Flirting with danger, Mom sat on the sofa next to Jack and gently sipped her coffee. I watched her closely and noticed slight changes in her. Mom wasn't the demure type, but she acted that way now, as though she wasn't sure how to act around a man who was so obviously taken with her.

Jack didn't touch his coffee. We were back to the deer-in-the-headlights look from him. I waved my hand in front of his face.

I glanced at Palmer, who didn't seem to know how to break the spell Jack had fallen into, either.

"I've shared with Mom how much I love Ponder," I said, hoping to start the conversation.

"Yes, and I was telling my daughter that I couldn't imagine living in such a desolate location—or her, for that matter."

I could almost feel Palmer stiffen and shoot a look my way, clearly wanting to defend the home that he loved back in Alaska. I stopped him with a smile that assured him I would see to that myself.

"I was telling Mom," I continued, "how I grew

accustomed to the isolation. There's a peacefulness and a beauty that I haven't found anywhere else. The town is tiny, I know, but the friends I made are the type who will last a lifetime. We rely on each other, help each other. You're right, Mom, it is nothing like Seattle or any big city, but it has its own character and its own appeal. I miss Ponder more than I ever thought I would." More accurately, I missed Palmer, but missing Ponder was no exaggeration on my part. I noticed Palmer's body language relax after I spoke.

"I like Seattle just fine," Jack said, looking directly at my mother. "Don't suppose you happen to know what the job prospects are like here for a hunting and fishing guide?"

"I don't," Mom told him.

"Never did any other kind of work, but I can whittle."

"You whittle, Jack?" I asked. The man was full of surprises.

"I do. Carved plenty of bear figurines over the years. I could set up a table at that market place you took me to and sell figurines . . . that is, if I had reason to live in Seattle."

"I thought crowds bothered you," Palmer reminded him.

"Gotta admit they do," Jack said, "but there's

adjustments a man needs to make for a woman who's captured his heart—especially if she refuses to live in Alaska."

I gestured toward Palmer, letting him know I agreed with Jack. I couldn't have said it any better myself. Not that I expected Palmer to move to Seattle.

Moving closer to me, Palmer sat on the arm of my chair. "I tend to agree."

"You do?" I whispered, my heart reacting in a crazed fashion.

"I've been looking at property in Fairbanks. It's close enough to drive there in fifteen to twenty minutes and far enough outside of town not to feel the world crowding in on us." He reached for my hand and gripped it with his own, intertwining our fingers.

I looked up and blinked at him, my eyes filled with warmth and love. If we were alone I would have reached up and kissed him.

"You been to Alaska?" Jack asked Mom.

"No, sorry to say, I never visited, although I've heard a lot of things about how beautiful it is, especially where those cruise ships go. Have you ever been on a cruise, Jack?"

Palmer coughed, sounding like he was close to losing a lung. Like him, no way could I picture Jack on a cruise ship.

Mom looked with concern at Palmer. "You okay?"

"Fine," he muttered, eyes watering as he blinked hard.

Jack set his mug aside. "I'm going to ask you something, Gina, and I need the truth."

He sounded serious. I was afraid of where this conversation was headed. Palmer must have shared my concern, because his hand tightened around mine.

Jack turned sideways to look directly at my mother. "I need to know, Gina, do you have a love interest?"

Startled, Mom swallowed hard, and I could tell the question troubled her. She blinked several times and sent a guilty look my way, confirming that I had reason for my suspicions. There *was* someone in my mother's life. Someone important. Her face said it all.

When she didn't answer, I prompted her. "Mom? You don't need to worry if you've met someone who interests you."

"You mean me?" Jack asked, hopeful.

"I have a friend," she admitted reluctantly, breaking eye contact with me. "A male friend."

"That's wonderful," I assured her.

"Craig and I have been seeing each other for a few months now."

"Craig?" Jack repeated in a devastated cry.

"Have I met him?" I didn't remember ever meeting anyone with that name.

"We were in Leavenworth together," Mom countered. "I know this is a shock to you. I wanted to tell you, I really did. I don't know why I held back . . . I guess I was afraid you'd disapprove."

"Mom, I would never do that."

"I've never been with anyone like Craig. Falling in love scares me. I was afraid to tell you, for fear it would all fall apart."

"Craig beat me out?" Jack wailed and buried his face in his hands.

"Honey, can we talk about this later?" Mom pleaded, just as the doorbell rang.

"Are you expecting anyone?" I asked her. A startled look flashed across her face as she stood to answer the door.

The three of us watched as Mom hesitantly crossed the room. When she opened the door, I saw an attractive, tall man with a full head of white hair on the other side. The two of them were whispering heatedly.

I could hear only part of the conversation.

"Now is not a good time," Mom insisted.

"You always say that. Gina, if you don't want me to meet your daughter . . ."

I couldn't hear the rest of the exchange.

Finally, Mom opened the door to allow the man to enter.

"Everyone, Josie, I'd like to introduce you to my . . . friend, Dr. Craig Hunt."

"Friend?" Craig whispered to my mom, his white brows arching with the question.

Jack released another wild cry of despair and fell against the back of the sofa.

Craig looked at Jack. "Do you need medical attention?" he asked.

"No, my friend's perfectly fine," Palmer said, sitting down next to Jack. "Give him a bit of time to recover and he'll be good as new."

The physician didn't appear convinced.

Mom was keeping a close eye on my reaction. I left my chair and came over to hug her and then stuck out my hand to Dr. Hunt. "I'm Josie, Gina's daughter, and I can't tell you how pleased I am to meet you . . . at last."

Craig Hunt grinned, and we impulsively hugged. I was happy for my mother and hoped she would be happy for me when I explained that I'd had a change of plans in my own life.

CHAPTER SIXTEEN

Palmer

Our dinner with Josie and her mother hadn't gone the way I'd wanted it to. Jack's behavior was bad enough, followed by the unexpected introduction of Gina Avery's male friend.

The doctor's arrival had come as a surprise to us all. Although I hated to leave, I needed to get Jack out of the house before he made a bigger fool of himself, even if it meant missing the dessert Josie had made for us. It did my heart good to see that she didn't want me to go; I was reluctant, too.

Before leaving, I arranged to meet her the following day to talk about our future. I loved her, but I'd had enough of this big-city life to last me for another two years.

Jack was beside himself, suffering with the loss of the supposed love of his life. His words, not mine. I'd had to talk him down once we got to the hotel, which wasn't easy. He seemed determined to win Gina's heart until I calmly explained that it looked like she'd already given it to another.

I'd told Josie I'd stay in Seattle for Christmas, but considering all that had happened, I wasn't sure if it was a good idea. Josie seemed intent on finding a new job in town, which implied she wasn't ready to make a commitment to us. I'd already mentioned the property I planned to purchase outside of Fairbanks with the hope she'd view that as a compromise. If matters didn't go as planned when we talked, and every indication told me she wasn't ready to leave Seattle, then I would rebook my ticket back to Alaska earlier instead of later. The tranquility of Ponder had never called to me louder or clearer. Seattle had way too many people and too much drama for me.

Josie had suggested we meet at a restaurant close to the hotel, which suited me. Jack hadn't left his hotel room since we'd returned from dinner at Josie's. I'd tried talking sense into him, but he'd spent the remainder of the night bemoaning his great loss until I couldn't take listening to him any longer and headed back to my own room.

Now I sat waiting in the restaurant Josie had recommended, reviewing in my mind all that I wanted to say to her. I arrived early and was able to get a booth, thinking that would give us more privacy than a table in the middle of a crowded restaurant. Josie arrived exactly on time. The instant I saw her walk in the door, I felt my heart squeeze with longing. I desperately wanted her in my life. After everything that had happened in the last couple days, I wasn't sure if it would ever come to be.

The hostess escorted Josie to the booth. She smiled and slid into the bench across from me.

After she removed her coat and gloves, she looked over and smiled. Immediately I felt better.

"Everything okay at home?" I asked.

She released a soft sigh. "Yes. Mom and I were finally able to talk. She's so in love with Craig, and for the little bit of time the three of us were together, I could see he feels the same way about her. I don't know why she wasn't comfortable enough to tell me about him. He's a widower, and he and Mom have a lot in common. I'm sincerely happy for her."

"So you like him?"

"I do. He apologized to me for showing up uninvited. He didn't know Mom had invited you and Jack to dinner. He'd come to meet me. It had frustrated him that she was keeping him a secret from me. Apparently, it had caused a rift between them. Mom had promised to introduce us when I first arrived back from Ponder but kept putting him off with one excuse after another until he took matters into his own hands.

"After you and Jack left, he apologized for barging in," Josie continued. "Mom had mentioned that I'd quit my job. He assumed I'd be at the house, and he was right. What he didn't expect was to walk into the middle of our dinner party."

"Jack's behavior didn't help matters any."

"The way he carried on was crazy. How is he today?"

Resisting the urge to laugh was almost impossible. "Last night he claimed that your mother was the love of his life and he will forever grieve the loss."

"Poor guy."

"He hasn't come out of his room, but don't worry, he had room service deliver his breakfast. From what I understand, it took two people to bring up his order."

The cheerful server stopped by with a list of specials for the day and took our drink order. Frankly, I didn't have much of an appetite. Josie didn't appear to have one, either. We each chose a salad.

"I suppose I should be more sympathetic toward

Jack claiming he's lost the love of his life." I picked up my fork to examine the tines, to be sure they were even.

"Jack isn't serious about Mom, is he?" Josie asked.

"He'll recover."

"I feel bad for him."

"Me, too." And I did. "I suggested that the strong attraction he felt for your mother was a sure sign he was ready to bring a woman into his life. I urged him to check out one of those online dating sites."

Josie's eyes grew dark and serious, as if the thought brought on a case of anxiety. "Have you ever tried one of those sites, Palmer?"

I found the question humorous. "Me on a dating site? No." I shook my head. "You?"

"No," she said, and then, in an apparent effort to update me on her job situation, she added, "You might be interested to hear Chef Anton contacted me."

Learning that came as no surprise. I struggled to hide my irritation. I figured it wouldn't take him long to admit he needed her and wanted her back. I was curious to find out what he was willing to do to get her to agree to return. "Did he offer you a raise?"

"No, quite the opposite. He assured me I wouldn't work in this town again."

The man was an idiot not to recognize what a jewel he had in Josie. "He's blackballing you?"

"He can try, but I sincerely doubt it will work. Besides, I've been having second thoughts about restaurant work altogether. The hours are brutal. The long days and my inability to create, combined with my awful experience with Chef Anton, have really soured my views of a career in this field."

"But you applied for other restaurant work," I reminded her. That had been the most discouraging news of my visit.

"I did, but out of obligation."

"Obligation?"

"Mom and I worked hard to pay for my culinary degree, and I felt I needed to give it another shot." She hesitated before adding, "Then I realized that this isn't what I want after all. I want to do more with my talent, more than directing other staff in a hot kitchen or being responsible for preparing other chefs' recipes."

My spirits elevated. This was exactly what I'd been wanting to hear before I brought up the idea of us marrying. Silence hung in the air until I approached the subject of us.

"Do you think you'd be happy working at the lodge

again next season?" I asked, unable to hide how anxious I was for her answer.

A slight frown marred her smile. "I don't know if it will be enough for me, Palmer."

There was a lull in the conversation and our salads were delivered. Neither of us reached for our forks.

"Are you saying you have no desire to return to Ponder?" I asked. I might as well get the question out in the open. If I was beating my head against a brick wall, then I needed to know it now. It was more like beating my *heart* against a brick wall.

"You heard me defend Ponder last night," Josie reminded me.

"Yes, but you didn't say you wanted to live there."

The warmth in her eyes told me everything. Everything that I needed to know—that she loved me. My heart pounded so loudly that I couldn't hear myself speak.

Looking down, Josie smoothed the cloth napkin across her lap. "If I had a good reason, Palmer, I'd go back to Ponder."

I stretched my arm across the table and took hold of her hand. "I know how badly I messed up the first time I asked you to marry me. I love you, Josie. You deserve all the right romantic words, and more than anything,

I wish I could give you all that and more. But that's not me. I'm just a guy who can't imagine not having you in my life. When you came to Ponder it felt like I'd found the one person in the world who would complete me. I couldn't wait to spend time with you. Being with you was the best part of my day. My work is my passion, or it was until I met you. You're everything to me. I'd hoped I'd showed you that by helping you get back to Seattle for your job. Your happiness is important to me. *You're* important to me."

"You're important to me, too."

"I wanted you to miss me and reconsider my proposal."

"Marrying you and living in Ponder wasn't an easy decision. I needed that time away. I had to give my dream a chance to find out if it was what I'd always hoped it would be. It wasn't, and I realized how much I loved you. Nothing was the way I'd imagined. Then things between us changed and I didn't know why. You didn't seem to have time for me any longer, and I didn't know what to think."

I was embarrassed to admit the truth. Seeing that we were both laying it all on the table, I had to be as honest with Josie as she was being with me. "I lost heart and felt it was best to own up to the fact that if I was losing you to Chef Anton, then the best thing to do was cut my losses."

"It was about that stupid Facebook post? Why didn't you ask me about it? If you had, I'd have explained everything. It was my first day on the job and I had no clue what I was getting myself into."

She brought up a good point. "I didn't feel I could," I admitted, "seeing that I was the one who insisted we not discuss the chef. Nor did I want you to feel like I'd become a stalker."

She laughed. "Palmer, honestly, reading my Facebook posts doesn't make you a stalker."

I was shaking inside, wanting her so badly. I wasn't sure what more I could say but felt I had to try. "You know I love you. If I knew any poetry, I'd recite it. If I could play the guitar, I'd serenade you. Sadly, I can't do either. All I can tell you is that my heart is yours if you want it, Josie."

She smiled that beautiful smile I loved so much. The smile that encouraged me.

I quickly added, "I want to make a life with you as my wife, and if you're willing to go a step further with me, I want to create a family with you."

I waited, wanting her to respond with a quick yes, but instead she was dabbing at her eyes with the linen napkin. "So," I said, releasing a deep breath, "which way are you leaning?"

Josie nodded.

"That's a yes?"

"Yes, Palmer, it's a resounding yes. What did you think I was telling you?"

I couldn't sit still. I jumped up from the booth and knelt beside her. Her warm hands framed my face and she leaned over and kissed me. It seemed the entire restaurant went strangely quiet, but I couldn't care less. I had everything I needed for a perfect Christmas. I had Josie.

After several kisses, Josie raised her head. "You better get up off your knees. People are looking at us."

I kissed the back of her hand and returned to my seat, jubilant and excited. Reaching across the table, we held hands, neither of us interested in our meals.

"We'd live in Ponder, right?" she asked.

"In-season, for sure. Off-season is negotiable. The property in Fairbanks looks promising. Where we live will be where you're the most comfortable, Josie, especially after we start a family."

"I so want children," Josie whispered.

"Me, too." I raised her hand to my lips and kissed her knuckles, unable to hold back. "I know you're passionate about your work. We'll find a way for you to use your talent and education, I promise you, Josie. Ponder isn't the end of the world; people still need to eat."

"Your faith in me means everything. I have confidence that I'll think of something: in fact, I have a couple ideas already. You should know, the way I feel right now, becoming your wife, sharing your life, making mine a part of yours, it's everything I would ever want or need."

My heart had settled down to a normal, steady beat, so I could breathe again. "Did I do better this time?" I asked. "With the proposal?"

"Much better, but I wouldn't mind you telling me again how much you admire my straight, white teeth."

Groaning, I shook my head. "I blame Jack for that fiasco."

"Then you should know your style of proposing is everything a woman could hope for from the man she loves."

"Thank you." I wasn't a quick study, but I did my best.

The server approached our table, and she noticed that neither of us had touched our meals. "Can I get either of you something different?" she asked.

I looked away from Josie for just a moment. "I think we're good. No," I corrected myself quickly, "on second thought, we'd like to order a bottle of champagne."

"Are you celebrating a special occasion?" she asked, having read the situation perfectly.

I doubt we could have fooled anyone in the vicinity around us.

"We're getting married."

The server's face lit up. "That's wonderful. Congratulations! A holiday proposal. It doesn't get any more romantic than that."

Josie

Three years later

I wrote down another ingredient and then went back to the stovetop and stirred the fresh ginger into the squash soup.

"Is it ready yet?" Jack asked. He sat at the kitchen counter, eagerly eyeing the pot on the burner.

"Give it a minute. I want the ginger to blend into it before you taste it."

Jack sat ready and waiting with a spoon clenched in his hand. He was always the first to try my recipes. My blog, which featured recipes with ingredients local to Alaska, had taken off, and I had a following of more than two hundred and fifty thousand now. The popularity had garnered the attention of several advertisers, who were seeking placement on my blog.

When Palmer and I married I'd wondered how I would be able to use my culinary degree living in a remote Alaskan location. Angie encouraged me to write a food blog.

In my first entry, I shared my recipe for moose stroganoff, along with the story of Jack the hunting guide and his love of food. I put it out on the Internet, not expecting much. Then Angie had reposted it to her own loyal following. The sharing and resharing turned it into something magical. Responses poured in, asking for more, and my audience had been growing ever since.

I called my blog *My Alaskan Holiday: Creating Amazing Dishes with the Bounties of Nature.* I'd never expected to bring in an income from writing about a subject that I dearly loved. I was astonished and speechless when the Cooking Channel contacted me about a possible television show featuring my recipes based on wild game, native fish, berries . . . all from Alaska, including stories about the nature all around us and our lifestyle in this remote burg. It was hard to believe that my life was coming together like this.

"It should be ready by now. Right?" Jack asked, interrupting my thoughts.

"Three more minutes," I told him. "Be patient. The soup will taste all the better. Remember, good things come to those who wait."

"I'm hungry."

"You're always hungry," I reminded him.

He grinned boyishly, his eyes sparkling. "I am, and you can count your blessings. If not for my love of your cooking, just where would you be?"

"True." Jack had encouraged me every step of the way.

It was a good life. Angie and Steve's little girl, Jaden, was three now, with two big brothers who protectively looked after her. My friend's writing career was booming as well. We'd grown closer than ever after my move to Ponder. She read and edited my blogs, and I was her first reader when it came to her novels.

Just as I was about to dish up Jack's soup, Donna arrived, after flying in from Fairbanks for spring break a day earlier. Jack had met her three years ago when he'd left Seattle, heading back to Alaska. Donna, a widow, taught in a school in Fairbanks and was in the middle seat next to Jack on his flight out of Sea-Tac. On the long flight to Fairbanks, Jack had been down in the dumps and was convinced he would forever mourn the loss of his one great love, my mother. Donna had kindly listened to Jack as he spoke of his heartache. She'd encouraged him to move on, and the two had exchanged contact information.

Before long, Jack was making any excuse he could find to fly into Fairbanks, and six months later, Jack and Donna were married. Donna continued to teach in Fairbanks but spent her school breaks and summers in Ponder with Jack. Jack stayed on as a hunting guide for the lodge, but all his off-season time was spent with Donna in Fairbanks. It worked for them, and it pleased me to see Jack happy and settled.

"I thought I'd find you here," Donna said to Jack as she strolled into the kitchen after a polite knock against the door.

"Josie made soup." He tilted his head to one side so Donna could kiss him. His beard was neatly trimmed these days, thanks to his wife's influence.

"Would you like a sample?" I asked her. "It's squash soup, from the squash I grew this summer." What most people didn't know was that with the long hours of daylight in the Alaska summers, the gardens served up a cornucopia of amazing and extra-large produce. It was a wealth of riches for me as a food blogger and a chef. Two of my most popular blog posts showed pictures of my garden and the incredible size of my squash and other vegetables.

"I've been fiddling with this recipe a bit and recently added—"

"Ginger," Donna finished for me. "The scent greeted me when I came through the door."

"Would you like a sample? I have plenty."

Donna pulled out a stool and joined Jack at the kitchen counter.

I dished up two bowls and took notes of their comments, knowing I would probably need to make a few adjustments. Jack, being Jack, rarely had a single suggestion. He would eat just about anything, which didn't make him my best critic. Nevertheless, I sought out his opinion, knowing he was always my biggest cheerleader. Donna, thankfully, was more discerning and made several observations that I found especially helpful.

When they'd finished with the soup, the two headed to the lodge. Since they'd married, Donna had become good friends with the Brewsters. She'd suggested adding a children's program to supplement what the lodge offered to families. Jerry and Marianne had jumped on the idea. Several young single college students had applied for positions, and Donna headed up the educational programs each summer.

In addition to writing my blog, I returned to the lodge as their chef. I'd found freedom and joy here that I hadn't expected; I was able to create and bring delight both to myself and to the guests and locals who ate at the lodge, all without the pressures I'd endured at the restaurant back in Seattle. My meals had even attracted the attention of several food critics, who wrote not only about the lodge and the food but the quaint town of Ponder. The Brewsters were already sold out for the next two years and were in the process of building small cabins to accommodate the growth in their business.

Ponder and the lodge weren't the only things experiencing growth and prosperity. Palmer had his own success. The Civil War sword he'd delivered before Christmas three years ago had caught the attention of reenactors and collectors, and my husband had received several other commissions. He'd been interviewed recently in a national magazine and had been part of a television competition, bringing home a ten-thousand-dollar prize. We'd used his winnings to add on to the house, in anticipation of expanding our family.

My mom was well and happy. She and Craig had married, less than a month after Palmer and I exchanged vows. I had come to admire and appreciate my stepfather. He was kind, generous, and levelheaded, and brought wonderful qualities to the marriage. They were blissfully happy. Craig was semiretired, which gave them time to travel. Last winter they'd taken a cruise in the South Pacific, starting in Hawaii and ending in Australia. They had recently returned from their second winter cruise, which took them to South America. Knowing my mother, she'd bought yarn while she was in Peru, as she was an avid knitter.

Just after noon, Palmer wandered into the kitchen, his heated face still red from working over his forge. "Is lunch ready?" he asked. He hesitated when he saw my face. "What's the problem—did you burn the soup?"

"No."

"It smells wonderful. What is it?" he asked. He stood in front of the stove and waved his hand over the pot. Leaning forward, he closed his eyes and breathed in the scent.

"It's ginger," I supplied.

"Yes, that's it," he concurred, taking in another deep breath. He opened his eyes and frowned. "Is something wrong? You look like you've got something up your sleeve. I know that look."

"Remember those pregnancy tests I asked Donna to bring from Fairbanks?"

Palmer went still and quiet. "I remember," he said softly.

"I used one this morning."

"And?"

"And we're pregnant."

Silence followed, and for an instant I was afraid Palmer wasn't happy with my news. That was before he let out a yell that shook the rafters. He gripped me around the waist and lifted me up in his arms, far off the ground.

"Palmer, Palmer, put me down."

I should have known better than to protest. It only encouraged him. Before I knew it, we were sitting on the sofa and I was in his lap. His large, muscular hands framed my face as he brought his mouth to mine, kissing me with a tenderness that still held the power to stir me.

With my arms wrapped around his neck, I kissed him back and then rested my head against his shoulder. "Are you happy?"

"You mean you can't tell? Think I'm more surprised than anything. It happened so fast. I thought these things took more time."

I'd been off birth control only a short while, and I was surprised myself with how quickly we'd conceived. "Me, too."

"I thank God every day you agreed to marry me, Josie. Every single day."

"And I thank God you were persistent, Palmer." I was unable to imagine what my life would be without him. Like Angie had realized when she moved to Ponder, I, too, discovered that what I gained here by far outweighed anything I now lived without.

Life was good. No, life was *great*. I was blessed. My Alaskan holiday had turned into so much more than I'd ever dreamed it could be.

Did you love *Alaskan Holiday*?
Read on for a sneak peek of
Debbie Macomber's bestselling
Christmas novel…

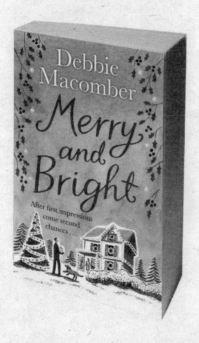

Filled with warmth, humour
and the promise of love…

CHAPTER ONE

*

Merry

"Mom, I need to work overtime, so I won't be home to help with dinner."

"Again?" her mother moaned into the phone.

"Yes, sorry." Merry hated leaving her mother with the task of cooking dinner. Robin Knight struggled with mobility issues due to complications with multiple sclerosis. As much as Merry hated the thought of it, her mother would soon be confined to a wheelchair.

"That's three nights this week."

Merry didn't need the reminder. Three nights out of four. Matterson Consulting, the firm where she worked as a temp, was involved in a huge project, its biggest one to date, for the Boeing company. With the time crunch, everyone on staff was putting in mandatory overtime. Normally, few would object to the extra hours, but the holiday season was right around the corner. People were busy planning parties, shopping for gifts, decorating, baking, and making holiday plans to visit families. All the normal, fun things that were part of this time of year, but for those employed by Matterson, it didn't matter. Christmas might as well be blocked off the calendar.

"Don't worry, dear," Merry's mother assured her gently. "Patrick will help me with dinner."

Merry closed her eyes and let her shoulders sag. Patrick was a dear boy, but he tended to dirty every dish in the house when he cooked. Her eighteen-year-old brother, who had Down syndrome, was the light of her life, but his help in the kitchen was questionable at best.

"Heat up soup and have Patrick make sandwiches," Merry suggested.

"We can do that, but you should know Bogie is out of dog food."

Bogie was Patrick's golden retriever, who had an appetite that rivaled that of an entire high school football squad. Grocery shopping was a task Merry had taken on as her mother's illness progressed. However, working the hours she did made it nearly impossible to find the time needed. "Oh Mom, I'm sorry. Poor Bogie.

I'll stop off at the store on my way home and pick some up." While she was there she'd grab a few other essentials, too, like milk and bread. They were running low on both. And maybe some ice cream for Patrick, who never complained about the need to help his mother.

"Your father can do that on his way home—"

"Don't ask Dad," Merry interrupted. Her father was in pharmaceutical sales and traveled extensively around the Pacific Northwest and was often on the road. He carried a heavy enough load as it was. By the time he got home from driving across the state, he'd be exhausted. Merry didn't want to burden him with any extra chores. Buying the groceries was her responsibility.

Everyone worked together in the Knight family. They were a tight-knit group by necessity and by love. Merry had taken the twelve-month temp job with Matterson Consulting to save tuition money for college. Her educational expenses were more than their family budget could manage. She'd been hired by Matterson Consulting specifically for this Boeing project and had worked extensively on inputting the data. It'd taken months to accumulate all the necessary information. It was all winding down now. December 23 would be her last day on the job.

After working with the company for nearly a year,

she'd made friends with the other two women working in data entry. They considered her part of the team and often turned to her with questions, as she had replaced the department head. Although she was only a temporary employee, her skill level was above those currently assigned to the project.

Merry took another bite of the peanut-butter sandwich she'd brought for lunch. She usually ate at her desk and worked through her lunch break. Most everyone else went to a local café around the corner, where the food was fast, cheap, and tasty. All three were necessary if Merry was going to splurge and eat out. She treated herself once a week, but more often than that would play havoc with her budget. Most days she brown-bagged it.

"When was the last time you went out, Merry?" her mother asked.

"I go out every day," she answered, sidestepping the question.

"On a date."

"Mom! When do I have time to date?" Merry had a fairly good idea what had prompted the question. Her best friend from high school, Dakota, had recently announced she was pregnant.

"That's exactly my point. You're twenty-four years old and you're living the life of a nun."

"Mom!"

"Patrick dates more than you do."

Merry had to smile, even though her mother was right. Her younger brother was involved with a special group that held dances and other events that allowed him to socialize with other teens who had Down syndrome. As a high school senior, he was active in drama and part of the football team. He had a girlfriend as well.

"It's time you stopped worrying about your family and had some fun."

"I have fun," Merry countered. She had friends, and while she didn't see them often, they were in touch via social media, email, and texting. If Merry was busy, which she tended to be, then she communicated with emojis. It was fun to see how much she could say with a simple symbol or two.

"Have you ever thought about joining one of those online matchmaking sites?" her mother asked, sounding thoughtful.

"No," Merry returned emphatically. She hoped the state of her social life would change once she could afford to return to school. It wasn't like she was a martyr, but at times she struggled with the weight of family obligations. She tried not to think about everything she was missing that her friends enjoyed. It was what it was, and it didn't do any good to feel sorry for herself. Her family needed her.

"Why don't you try it? It'd be fun."

"Mom, have you seen all the forms and question-naires that need to be filled out for those dating sites? I don't have time for that." *Especially now, with the demands of my job,* she thought to herself.

"Make time."

"I will someday," she said, hoping that would appease her mother.

"Someday, Merry? Failing to plan is planning to fail."

"Mom. You sound like Tony Robbins." Although she complained, her mother was right. The timing, however, was all wrong.

"I'll think about it after the first of the year," she promised.

Dakota had met the love of her life online at Mix and Mingle. Inspired by her success, Merry had checked out the site, but she became bogged down with the page upon page of questions that needed to be completed. She started filling out the forms but quickly gave up, exasperated by all the busywork.

"You need to get out more, enjoy life," her mother continued. "There's more to life than work and more work."

"I agree. After the holidays. Let me finish this temp job first."

"It worked for Dakota."

"Mom, please. I have plenty of time to get out there." Merry didn't need the reminder about her friend's happy ending. After Dakota met Michael on the site, she had sung the website's praises to Merry like a wolf howling at the moon. She wouldn't stop bugging Merry about it until she'd promised to give it a try.

"I heard from her mother this morning. Did you know Dakota and Michael are expecting?"

"Yes, Mom, I heard." Merry reached for her sandwich and was about to take another bite when the vice president of the company, Jayson Bright, walked past her desk. He had to be one of the most serious-minded men Merry had ever met. To the best of her memory, she had never seen the man smile. Not once. He looked about as happy as someone scheduled for a root canal.

Jayson Bright paused and stared at Merry. His eyes fell to the nameplate on her desk. MARY KNIGHT. She'd asked HR to correct the spelling of her first name twice, with no success, and then gave up. Seeing that she was a temp, they hadn't shown that much interest. Her boss's gaze landed on the sandwich she had on her desk, and for a moment she toyed with the idea of offering him half, but as she doubted he'd find any humor in it, she restrained herself. He arched his brows before he walked away.

"Merry, did you hear me?" her mother asked.

"Sorry, no, I was distracted." From Mr. Bright's look, Merry had to wonder if there was something written in the employee handbook about eating at her desk. She'd been doing it for almost a full year now, and no one had mentioned that it was frowned upon before.

"Merry?"

"Mom. I need to get off the phone. I'll call you before I leave the office."

"Okay, but think about what I said, all right?"

"I will, Mom." Merry's mind filled with visions of meeting her own Prince Charming. Of one thing she was certain: It wouldn't be someone as dour as Jayson Bright.

Sure enough, just as Merry suspected, at three that same afternoon, a notice was sent around the office.

It is preferred that all staff refrain from eating at their desks. For those who choose to remain in the office for lunch, a designated room is provided. Thank you.

Jayson Bright
Vice President
Matterson Consulting

Merry read the email and instinctively knew that this edict was directed at her. She preferred to avoid the lunchroom, and with good reason. The space was often crowded, and it was uncomfortable bumbling around, scooting between those at the tables and those waiting in line for a turn at the microwave. Besides, it was more efficient to eat at her desk. Not that Mr. Bright seemed to notice or care.

What a shame—the company vice president was such a curmudgeon. Merry had heard women in the office claim he was hot. She agreed. Jayson Bright was hot, all right. Hotheaded! He was young for his position as vice president. The rumor mill in the office said he was related to the Matterson family; the company president was his uncle. Bright would assume the role when it came time for his uncle to retire. His uncle would continue as chairman of the board.

Merry's thoughts drifted to Jayson Bright, and she mused at how attractive he would be if he smiled. He was about six feet tall, several inches taller than her five-five, with dark brown hair and eyes. He kept his hair cut in a crisp professional style. Wanting to be generous in spirit, Merry supposed he carried a heavy responsibility. Word was that Jayson Bright was the one responsible for obtaining this Boeing contract. A lot weighed in the balance for him with his job. Merry knew that he put in as many hours, or more, as the rest of the staff.

By the time Merry arrived at home, hauling a ten-pound bag of Bogie's favorite dog food, it was after eight o'clock. As soon as she walked in the door, Patrick rushed to help her with the heavy sack.

His sweet, boyish face was bright with enthusiasm. "Merry's home," he shouted, taking the dog food out of her hands and carting it to the kitchen pantry.

"Hi, sweetheart," her mother called. Her mom leaned heavily on her walker, now exhausted and fatigued, because she grew tired at the end of each day.

"Can I tell her?" Patrick asked excitedly.

"In a minute," her mother said. Merry noticed that her lips quirked in an effort to hold in a smile.

"Tell me what?"

"We got you an early birthday gift this afternoon and it's the best one ever." Patrick rubbed his hands together, unable to disguise his eagerness.

"You did?" Knowing the family budget was tight, Merry wasn't expecting much. Born on December 26, the day after Christmas, Merry had felt cheated as a child when it came to her birthday gifts. Her parents had done their best to make her birthday special, but it being so soon after Christmas made that difficult. It wasn't unusual for Merry to get her birthday gifts early because of it.

"And you're going to be so happy," Patrick assured her. "I helped Mom with everything."

"You helped pick it out?" Merry asked. The two of them must have ordered something off the Internet, because her mother was no longer able to drive and Patrick couldn't. Those with Down syndrome could legally drive in Washington State, but the family couldn't afford a second car. The family had only the one car, which her father used for work. Merry used public transportation to and from her job.

"Well, this isn't something we picked out. You need to do the picking."

"Patrick," his mother chastised. "You're going to give it away."

"You can show me after you feed Bogie," Merry suggested, as Bogie eyed the pantry door.

"We can't really give it to you yet," Patrick told her. "You get to choose for yourself, but I'll help if you want." From the way his eyes lit up, Merry knew he'd be terribly disappointed if he didn't get a say in this.

Okay, now Merry was willing to admit she was

intrigued. It was still November, over Thanksgiving weekend. Her brother was barely able to contain himself, and he rushed to grab Bogie's food dish. She enjoyed his enthusiasm. Seeing the happy anticipation in him piqued her own. She couldn't imagine what this special birthday gift could possibly be.

Bogie pranced around in his eagerness for Patrick to fill the dish so he could eat.

"Now, Mom, now?" Patrick asked, jumping up and down after he poured the dog food into the bowl. Between the dog and her brother, the two looked like they were doing a square dance.

"Let me eat dinner first," Merry said, teasing her brother.

Patrick's eyes rounded. "Merry, no, please. I've been waiting and waiting to tell you. I don't think I can wait any longer." Merry and her mother shared a smile.

"Have pity on the boy," her mother urged.

Holding back a smile would have been impossible. "Okay, Patrick, you can tell me about my birthday gift."

Her brother's eyes lit up like Fourth of July sparklers. Whatever this early birthday present was must be special. Merry hugged her brother and, wrapping her arms around his torso, gave him a gentle squeeze.

Patrick took hold of her hand while their mother

opened the laptop and pulled out a chair to sit down. Merry joined her mother.

"You ready?" Robin Knight asked, turning on the computer.

"I can hardly wait," Merry answered.

Tucking his arm around her elbow, Patrick scooted close to Merry.

She looked at the blank computer screen, getting more curious by the second. They both seemed to be squirming with anticipation. "What did you two order me?"

Patrick laughed and pointed to the computer, crying out, "We got you a *man* for your birthday!"

"What?" Merry asked, certain there was some misunderstanding. "I don't think it's possible to buy me a man."

"Not exactly buy," her mother explained. "Patrick and I spent the afternoon online, answering the questionnaire for Mix and Mingle. We filled in your profile and signed you up for the next six months."

Merry was speechless for several moments. *"You did what?"*

"We got you a date," Patrick answered, beaming her a huge smile.

If she wasn't already sitting, Merry would have needed

to take a seat. Her immediate thought was how best not to disappoint her mother and brother by telling them this wasn't anything she wanted. That thought was quickly followed by a question. "What photo did you use?" She hoped it was a recent one and not some high school prom picture. She'd changed a lot since her teen years. She wore contacts now instead of glasses, which showed off her deep brown eyes; her hair was longer now, shoulder length, parted in the middle. She'd be mortified if they'd used the photo on her employee badge for Matterson Consulting, where she looked like a deer caught in the headlights. Actually, it resembled more of a mug shot.

"That's the best part," Patrick told her, looking well pleased with himself. "We didn't use a photo of you."

Now Merry was totally baffled. "You mean to say you posted a picture of someone else?"

"Don't be silly," her mother responded.

"Well, if it isn't me, then whose photo did you use?"

Patrick's glee couldn't be contained. "We used Bogie's."

"You made me a dog?" Merry cried, resisting the urge to cover her face. "Why?"

"Two reasons," her mother explained.

"One," Patrick intervened, thrusting his index finger into the air, ready to show his reasoning, "you love dogs."

"Ah . . . I guess," Merry admitted. Bogie was as much her dog as Patrick's. He often slept on her bed. She took him for walks on the days Patrick couldn't. Bogie was considered part of the Knight family.

"And second, and most important," her mother continued, "you're a beautiful young woman. Too many potential dates would judge you purely on your looks. That didn't sit right with me. I wanted them to get to know you as a person, as the generous, kindhearted, loving woman you are. They will need to dig deeper into your profile rather than to simply gaze at a photograph. And," she added, "we weren't sure how you'd feel about all of this, so we chose a pseudonym for your name. You are now Merry Smith."

"Merry Smith," she repeated slowly, still having trouble taking all this in. Looking at her profile as it came up on the screen, she withheld a groan. After seeing Bogie with her pseudonym listed below, she figured it was highly unlikely anyone would send her a Mix and Mingle message. Anyone looking at the photo would think her profile was all one big joke. No one wanted to date a dog.

Want to know what happens next?

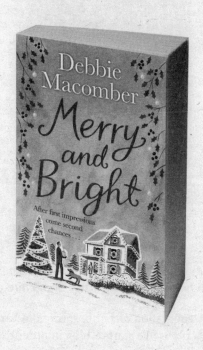

ORDER YOUR COPY NOW

Available in paperback
and e-book

Twelve Days of Christmas

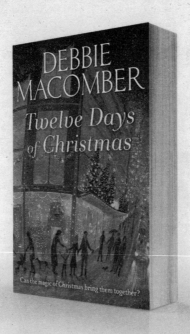

Julia is infuriated by her grumpy neighbour, **Cain**, who can't even be pleasant when they bump into each other.

So on the suggestion of her best friend, Cammie, Julia concocts a plan. She starts a blog in order to clinch her perfect job, and now she has a subject. Over the next twelve days, she is going to kill Cain with kindness – and Christmas cheer – and document it for all to read about.

But as the experiment goes on, Julia realises she underestimated the effect it would have on Cain, and on their relationship, and things take an unexpected turn . . .

Available to buy in paperback and ebook

Dashing Through the Snow

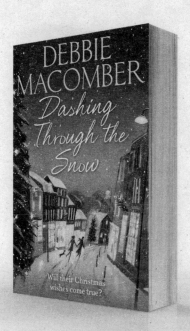

This Christmas will be full of surprises…

All that **Ashley** wants for Christmas is to get home to surprise her widowed mother. But all the flights are booked and there's only one car left to hire.

Dash is in a hurry. Newly demobbed from the army, he has an interview to attend, and he's determined to get the job. If getting there means sharing a car with the extremely talkative Ashley, then that's what he'll have to do.

The last thing either of them expected was that they may begin to like each other…

Available to buy in paperback and ebook

Mr. Miracle

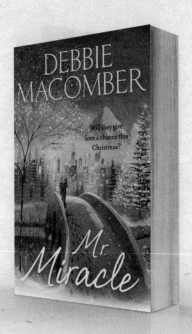

Harry Mills is a guardian angel on a mission: help **Addie Folsom** to get her life back on track – and help her find love.

Creating a happy ending for Addie and her neighbour Erich doesn't seem like much of a challenge. But soon after arriving in the town of Tocoma, Harry realises he might need some guidance. Addie and Erich can't stand each other: growing up he was popular and outgoing, while she was rebellious and headstrong. Addie would now rather avoid Erich entirely, especially at Christmas.

Harry is going to need all the help he can get, and a bit of divine inspiration, to help Addie and Erich find their Christmas miracle.

Available to buy in paperback and ebook

Starry Night

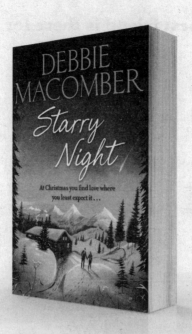

Carrie Slayton, a big-city society- page columnist, longs to write more serious news stories. So her editor hands her a challenge first: Carrie must score the paper for an interview with **Finn Dalton**, the notoriously reclusive author.

Living in the Alaskan wilderness, Finn has written a bestselling book about surviving in the wild. But he declines to speak to anyone, and no one knows exactly where he lives. With her career at stake, Carrie sacrifices her family celebrations and flies out to snowy Alaska.

When she finally finds Finn, she discovers a man both more charismatic and more stubborn than she expected. And soon Carrie is torn between pursuing a story of a lifetime and following her heart.

Available to buy in paperback and ebook

A best friend is there for you

Spring

Spring is full of Blossom Street and New Beginnings

BLOSSOM STREET

Starting Now

Blossom Street Brides

NEW BEGINNINGS

Last One Home

A Girl's Guide to Moving On

If Not for You

Winter

Curl up with a Christmas classic

Angels at the Table

Starry Night

Mr Miracle

Dashing Through the Snow

Twelve Days of Christmas

Merry and Bright

Discover your next Debbie Macomber

through all the seasons

Summer

Spend the summer a world away . . .

ROSE HARBOR

The Inn at Rose Harbor

Rose Harbor in Bloom

Love Letters

Silver Linings

Sweet Tomorrows

A ONE OFF

Any Dream Will Do

Cottage by the Sea

Autumn

These Rose Harbor ebook short stories
are the perfect mini break

When First They Met

Lost and Found in Cedar Cove

Falling for Her

Meet friends you'll call family

Stay friends with Debbie Macomber

Join Debbie and your fellow fans online to chat and swap stories

/DebbieMacomberWorld

@debbiemacomber

@debbiemacomber

/debbiemacombervideos

Check out Debbie's website and sign up to her newsletter for all the latest news on her books, giveaways, recipes and much more.

www.debbiemacomber.com